D1738625

*And suddenly there was with the angel a multitude
of the heavenly host, praising God, and saying,
Glory to God in the highest, and on earth peace,
good will toward men.*

—LUKE 2:13–14 (KJV)

Savannah Secrets

Savannah Secrets

Jingle Bell Heist

Ruth Logan Herne

Guideposts

Danbury, Connecticut

Jingle Bell Heist

Chapter One

FOUR MILLION DESSERTS AND COUNTING...

Julia Foley didn't give her business partner and friend time to kick off her shoes inside the door on the early December Friday. She grabbed Meredith Bellefontaine by the hand and hustled her over to the basement stairs. On the way down, she indicated the two plastic containers in Meredith's hands with a quick look. "Thank you so much for doing these, Mere. It's a big help."

"Always happy to—"

Julia turned when Meredith stopped talking.

Eyes wide, Meredith had stalled on the middle stair.

She was staring at Julia's finished basement.

Julia had set up long portable tables to help organize the church's annual Christmas bake sale. Each table was covered with stacks of plasticware, and each container held delicious desserts, guaranteed to please.

Meredith swallowed hard then came down the last few steps. "Julia, the New Beginnings baking committee has outdone themselves."

It was Julia's turn to take a breath, but Meredith wasn't done. Her gaze swept the wide range of containers. "This is wonderful! The sale will be a huge success. No wonder you chair it. How can I help you organize?"

Meredith's dive-in nature was exactly what Julia needed right now. "I want to tag everything, transport it to the hall, and have it ready for tomorrow because I've got the Christmas Box Fund meeting on Tuesday night and I need to get my notes ready for that."

"Another wonderful cause." Meredith smiled as she set her plastic containers down. "Should we load up the car and drive these over?"

"After we go through my checklist." Julia handed Meredith a steno-style notepad and a pencil. "I want your opinion on the selection to see if anything's missing. Okay?"

Meredith flipped the notepad open. "I can't imagine we're missing a thing, but I'm ready. Let's go."

Julia tapped the first group of containers. "Carrot cake with cream cheese frosting, carrot cake with pineapple and walnuts and cream cheese frosting, and carrot cake with raisins and walnuts and the ubiquitous—"

"Cream cheese icing." Meredith laughed. "You can never have too much carrot cake or too much icing. Done."

"Four harvest apple cakes with burnt sugar icing, three oatmeal cakes with broiled coconut topping, and six of Grandma Waverly's fruitcake loaves for the stouthearted among us."

"I refuse to waste my calories on something as odious as fruitcake," said Meredith as she jotted things down. When she was done, she indicated a stack to her left. "But are those six containers all pralines? Who made them? You know that pralines and fudge are my downfall."

"I made them," Julia said when Meredith looked up from her list.

"You've been busy."

Meredith didn't know the half of it, and Julia was embarrassed to have her know, but Meredith had been her friend for a long time.

"And we have twelve-and-a-half-dozen chocolate chip cookies, minus one as payment." Meredith grinned as she savored a bite of the cookie she'd filched. "It's my pleasure to be the official taste tester. Are these Wanda's contribution?"

"Her recipe, yes."

A tiny furrow deepened between Meredith's brows as Julia pointed out two more plastic containers and said, "Lemon bars, a wretchedly awful thing for December, but at the request of Mortie Sims, and considering his age, I made them."

Meredith's pencil paused.

She glanced right. Then left. Then right again. "Jules, did you make all this?"

Reckoning had come.

Julia swallowed a sigh. "Mostly. Yes. Except the things you just brought and three others."

"Julia, why?" Meredith didn't just look surprised. She looked shocked by the revelation. "I know New Beginnings isn't a huge congregation, but there are so many people willing to help. Why did all this fall on you?" True concern deepened the lines between her friend's brows.

"It's December." Julia shrugged. "Everyone's busy. When a couple of folks bowed out because of the flu, I jumped in to make up lost ground. And then I didn't stop. It seemed easier than calling around, begging for help. Let's just say my freezer became a close personal friend this past week."

Meredith frowned. "Except that New Beginnings is about the sweetest church there is, and I'm sure Naomi is baking for the kids."

Naomi was their beloved pastor's organized and kindhearted wife.

"And Myla loves to make cream cheese brownies."

Myla worked for Meredith's neighbor Harlowe Green, the oldest citizen of the city of Savannah.

Julia cringed.

"You haven't asked them to help." Meredith's brows shot up. "Why?"

"We had a committee, and I thought we were all set. Then it turned out that a few of the members weren't all that motivated. I didn't realize that until this last week, and I didn't think it would be right to call folks in December when everyone has so many commitments. Except I did call you because I knew you'd drop everything to help."

Meredith looked unconvinced. She tipped her reading glasses down. "Why take this on yourself, my friend? At this time of year?"

The very question Julia had been asking herself all week. A question that had no answers. "I'm already avoiding the calendar because there are so many things that crop up this month. Former jobs, organizations, old friends, and neighbors all seem intent on hosting some kind of holiday gathering. We're booked each of the next two weekends and two Wednesdays, one Tuesday and one Thursday. And everyone expects either a dish to pass or a box of cookies for a cookie exchange."

Meredith's frown deepened. "That's crazy, Jules. To tie up that much time? Is that what you want? To be run ragged with things all through December?"

Julia wasn't sure herself.

Any other time of year she was the delegator. She handed out jobs left and right, spreading the joy of many hands making light work, but not in December. Never in December.

Meredith looked about to say something else, but she must have thought better of it because she paused, clamped her mouth shut, and went straight back to the list. "Let's get this done, and then we can pack the car. Next?"

"Chocolate frosted peanut butter."

"Those were Ron's favorite."

Ron Bellefontaine was Meredith's late husband. He'd begun an investigations agency decades before, an agency that Meredith and Julia reopened eighteen months ago—and what a wonderful year and a half it had been.

Julia really didn't want to be questioned about her reasoning, mostly because she hadn't figured it out herself. She'd been scolding herself for the last three days, a long seventy-two hours of baking, baking, baking. "Done." She pressed a label onto the large sealed plastic container and pointed to one of the containers Meredith had brought in.

"My totally Southern contribution of chocolate fudge bourbon balls, made famous by my late mother-in-law. The Bellefontaine family has declared them to be the best in the world, and as a young bride I learned to never argue with the Bellefontaine clan. In this case, they are probably right."

"Thank you for doing them." Julia pointed to another container. "And you did the fudge too?"

"Yes, ma'am, but looking at all you did I feel like a slacker." Meredith smiled as Julia labeled the plastic container before setting it aside for transport to the church hall.

Julia opened her mouth just as the doorbell pealed and her phone lit up with her doorbell app.

"You've got that linked to your phone?" asked Meredith. "Since when?"

"A few of Beau's friends have this app. He decided we couldn't live without it and installed one yesterday. I'm not sure how I feel about it." She glanced at her phone and recognized her neighbor. "Tasha, hey," she said. "I'm in the basement. I'll be right up."

"Do you want me to finish?" asked Meredith.

Julia shook her head and muted the app. "Let's have coffee. Tasha's had a rough few months, and she looks like she might be having a bad day."

"Coffee it is."

Julia led the way up the stairs, and when she opened the front door, her thirty-something neighbor almost fell through the opening. Eyes wide, Tasha Alexander glanced behind her as if checking for pursuers then shut the door snugly, flipped the deadbolt, and turned, ashen-faced.

"Tasha, what's happened? What's going on? Is it the boys?" Tasha had a seven-year-old and a nine-year-old, a pair of normal, busy boys. "Are they all right? Are you?" Julia asked as she turned to lead Tasha into the living room.

"My shoes!" Tasha pulled up short, aghast, a proper Southern woman to the max. "On your good rug? I can't even!"

"Everything here is washable," Julia reassured her, but she waited while Tasha toed off the cute boots she was wearing. "Are we good now?" she teased once the boots were squarely on the foyer throw rug.

"No." Tasha moved forward, sank onto the sofa, and put her head in her hands. "And maybe never will be again, but I didn't do it, Julia." Anguished, she dropped her hands, sighed, and looked straight at Julia while Meredith set up coffee in the kitchen. The open concept of the house left them visible to one another.

"Do you want privacy?" Julia posed the question softly. She would never hurt Meredith's feelings, but if Tasha had private news to share, Meredith would understand. "I'm sure Meredith—"

"No." Tasha shook her head. "I want you both here."

Julia glanced toward the kitchen.

Meredith arched both brows in silent question.

Julia shifted her attention back to her newest guest. "What's happened, Tasha?"

"A theft at the museum."

Meredith left the coffee to burble and moved closer.

"Someone stole something from the museum?" Julia liked history all right, but she didn't pretend to be a regular visitor to the beautiful historical museum sprawled out at the intersection of Liberty Street and Martin Luther King Jr. Highway. History was Meredith's forte. "I thought the museum was undergoing some kind of major renovation and closed to visitors?"

"They reopened the tours to drive up annual memberships for the coming year. Memberships are a big Christmas gift idea, and it should have been all right because the rough spots were cordoned off, but it wasn't all right." She sighed deeply. "It was bad from the beginning, and it shouldn't have been, even if this was the first one I've done all on my own. We were only fifteen minutes or so into it when the power went out. It was black as pitch in the areas with no windows because they didn't have the backup system rewired into the new system yet. So when we lost power, folks screamed and began yelling and running back and forth. It was a mess. It's an old multistory schoolhouse, so there are no big windows that give natural light in the entry like a modern museum might have. Without power and the emergency backup system there was hardly any light at all."

"So what happened?" Meredith moved into the room and took a seat.

Tasha shook her head. "I waited to make certain everyone had safely left the floor. One of our regular security guards, Jay Crawford, was up there too, and when it seemed like everyone was down the stairs, I met Jay. He followed me out and drew the rope across the stairs so no one could get back up there."

"Except a rope is only a visual reminder," Julia said. "Not an actual barrier."

"A good point, but Jay stayed there, watching, while I tried to calm the situation down. And when we finally got the lobby cleared and folks on their way, I went back upstairs with my cell phone flashlight. Jay has one of those bigger ones, and the construction foreman hooked up one of their big lights. Jay and I looked around. Everything looked fine until we got to the Settled in Savannah holiday exhibit." Tears welled in her eyes.

Julia handed her a wad of tissues from a nearby box. "Here, sweetie. What happened then?"

"The bells were gone." She took a deep breath, squared her shoulders, and faced Julia and Meredith. "The Mulholland bells, a forty-three piece set of handbells donated by St. Kieran's Church down near the water. Bells that were brought here in the mid-1800s as an act in P.T. Barnum's traveling show. Absolutely irreplaceable."

"Mulholland Laces & Wovens?" Julia exchanged a look with Meredith. Everyone knew of the rich local family, not just because of their Fortune 500 textile company but because of their constant infighting that had resulted in lawsuits and cross-claims over the years.

"The very same. They were individually made handbells in very nice condition. They were donated to the museum over a decade ago. But that's not the worst part." She clutched the tissues to her face for a moment then took another deep breath. "Councilman Webster is part of the family. Hank *Mulholland* Webster. And some of his own family members were in the crowd, heckling him. I'm sure you know how the Mulhollands don't all get along," Tasha explained. "My boss always double-checks whenever she displays something related to their family history because some might be fine with it, but a cousin or brother or aunt or uncle somewhere might launch an objection. They always seem to be at odds. Maybe if I'd had more experience with them, I'd have been better prepared for what happened. But I was completely taken by surprise when Fiona Mulholland showed up with a whole crew of people protesting the city spending hundreds of thousands of dollars on Christmas lights when soup kitchens need help. She was leading chants about that while her cousin was trying to gain support for the city's Toys on Patrol campaign. Then the lights go out and the family's heirloom bells go missing. I can't think of a worse possible coincidence."

Coincidence?

Or plan?

Julia exchanged a look with Meredith. "This is awful, Tasha, but you couldn't have foreseen this. Things happen."

"But that's just it." She brought the tissues to her face again. "The police took me into a back room for questioning because I was the last person up there, and I'm afraid they're going to think I did it, Julia."

"Why would they do that?" Tasha was a hardworking, honest woman who helped elderly neighbors and saved lost kittens. The thought of her pilfering a pricey collection of bells was ridiculous.

"Because I'm broke."

Her sad expression underscored her fear.

"This divorce is costing me my house and my car," she confessed. "I was close to staying afloat, but then the latest ruling said I had to hand over half of my inheritance from my grandmother because it doesn't matter that Hayden cheated on me, squandered money on high living on his 'business trips'"—she waggled quote marks with her fingers—"and has skipped all the important days in his sons' lives. It came down to when Meemaw died and how long we were married, which means the cushion I thought I had is gone. If they're looking for someone who needs money, Julia"—she lifted water-filled eyes—"I'm their number-one suspect. And I need your help."

Chapter Two

Julia glanced at Meredith.

Meredith nodded.

Julia reached for Tasha's hand. "Of course we'll help. Where are the boys?"

"With their father. Not by his choice," she added. Frustration thickened her voice. "His mother told him that if he didn't take the time to bring the boys to visit, she was done with him. I think she's as upset as I am. Wendy Alexander is a good woman who did her best under tough circumstances. Hayden was an only child, and she admits she may have indulged him too much, but you'd expect folks to grow up eventually, wouldn't you?" She sighed. "Anyway, Hayden has them overnight, and then they're spending a day making cookies with his mother tomorrow."

Tomorrow.

The bake sale.

Julia stood quickly. "Tasha, we'll be happy to help you, but I have to ask a favor first. I have half a million desserts downstairs that must be taken to my church for our annual bake sale. What are you doing right now?"

"Besides crying, wringing my hands, and gnashing my teeth?"

Meredith crossed the room and gave Tasha a hand up. "All of which can be done while delivering these baked goods." She beamed a bright smile at Tasha and hugged her arm. "Let's get this stuff where it needs to go. That'll keep you busy."

"Once we've got the containers delivered we can devote time to your concerns. Because you're right." Julia spoke with confidence. "It's either a coincidence that those bells disappeared during Councilman Webster's visit, or it's not, but a construction area is a great place to stage a robbery. Simply because there are so many things already out of place and disturbed."

"It is," admitted Tasha. "We're creatures of habit at the museum. We like everything in its place, unless we're changing an exhibit. So we were already distracted and out of sorts with the remodeling."

"Changes in scheduling can play tricks on us," noted Julia. She led the way to the basement and then pointed to a stack of clear plastic totes. "Let's load these up. Fortunately, I have two ladies organizing the tables at the church, so that part of my committee didn't fade out."

They got busy and toted nine ginormous plastic totes to Julia's car and Meredith's SUV. Even with two vehicles, it was a tight fit, but when they got to the church, the pair of women on set-up duty made quick work of emptying the cars.

Julia hesitated at the doorway leading into the parish life center. "Should we stay and help them get organized?" she whispered to Meredith.

Meredith's brows couldn't have shot higher. "No, we should not," she declared softly. "You've done enough. Hand over the reins. Good heavens, girl, this isn't like you. Usually you're the Queen of

Delegation, but it appears that the holiday season may be your Achilles' heel."

Tasha had delivered the final plastic tote to the hall.

Meredith was right.

Julia poked her head around the corner. "I'll see you gals tomorrow, okay?"

"See you then, Julia! Bye, Meredith!" One of the women waved. They'd already set up tables and had used cheerful holiday-themed cloths on each one. They'd even laid them out according to color patterns. Reds and greens on one side, golds, silvers, and ivory on another, and they'd used Christmas icons for the Annual Cookie Corner, where folks could buy one cookie or dozens.

"They're fine." Meredith indicated Tasha with a quick glance. "Office, your house, or mine?"

"The office." Julia kept her voice soft. "Most of our neighbors are wonderful, but there are a couple of busybodies. Once this news hits the TV and the internet, their tongues could start wagging. Let's minimize the ammunition. No one needs that, especially a single mom. Can you text Carmen to put on some coffee?"

"Sure will."

Tasha rode with Julia.

She was calmer now. Maybe it was sharing her fears with someone else or two of the best chocolate chip cookies in existence, but when they got to their renovated office space on Whitaker Street, she was much more composed.

Carmen greeted them as they came in. Carmen was Julia and Meredith's "gal Friday," and she was an amazing help. She indicated a fresh pot of coffee and a loaf of sliced sweet bread. "Courtesy of

Tay Tay Pomeroy," she announced. "It could use more cinnamon because a pumpkin spice bread should be spicy, but that might be my Latina roots showing. When Mamá cooked, spice meant spice."

Taylor "Tay Tay" Pomeroy was Meredith's hairstylist. Julia smiled. "How wonderfully thoughtful of her."

"Oh, this is just the beginning," replied Carmen, but she paused as Julia introduced Tasha.

"Tasha, this is our extremely capable assistant, Carmen Lopez. She keeps us running smoothly. Carmen, Tasha Alexander is our newest client. She's also my neighbor. And what did you mean about it being a beginning?"

"Follow me, *amigas*." Carmen had been born in Guatemala. Her family had emigrated to America when she was young, but she'd lost her parents in a tragic accident. She'd run into Julia when she was on the wrong side of the law as a teen, and Julia had seen something special in the young girl. Now Carmen was grown up and not only working for Magnolia Investigations but was also a Big Sister to a seven-year-old little girl. Carmen Lopez was good people.

Carmen ticked her fingers as they moved to the office kitchen in the repurposed old home. "Cookies, cakes, and breads, courtesy of the Whitaker Business Association; Harlowe Green's housekeeper, Myla Thomas; Jubal Early Jones's daughter-in-law; and Maribelle at the diner. And the gorgeous evergreen centerpiece, the only inedible item in the current bunch, is courtesy of none other than Quin Crowley." She pretended to swoon and batted her eyes in Meredith's direction. "He sent them to the agency, but I think we all know who they're for."

Meredith blushed. "I'm sure Quin sent that for all of us to enjoy."

"This is so nice." Tasha looked at the buffet of treats surrounding the flowers on the old-fashioned table. "Folks appreciate you gals."

"That's about ten pounds' worth of appreciation right there," mused Meredith, but she slipped a pair of cookies from one of the covered trays. "Chocolate and peppermint," she noted, holding them up. "It's all about balance. Let's go through to the conference area."

They settled across the hall in what used to be Ron Bellefontaine's office. Meredith had lost her husband three years before under tragic circumstances. The suddenness of her loss left her reeling, but when she'd approached Julia about reopening the investigations agency, Julia had agreed. Meredith had the experience and the licensing, and Julia had been a Georgia court justice for years. They knew both sides of the law, and neither woman was ready to retire.

Carmen brought two large yellow pads to the room. She handed one to Meredith and one to Julia, then closed the door behind her when she left the room.

"Tasha, I want you to go over every detail of the day. When exactly did this happen?"

"Today."

Julia's jaw dropped. "Today as in today?"

Tasha nodded. Her eyes filled again. "Is that bad?"

Julia was about to write the date on the empty pad, but hesitated. "It's only two forty in the afternoon. How did all this happen and you were at my door an hour ago?"

"They shut us down and said to go home."

Meredith frowned. "Did the police interview you at the station also, or just at the museum?"

"Just at the museum. They asked what I knew. I said I know nothing. They asked what I saw. Also nothing. I wasn't much help to them. And I couldn't stop crying, so I think they just gave up after a while."

Julia inhaled then jotted down the date. "I'm sure they'll get back in touch. So from your perspective, let's go over the day. You said there was a gathering."

"Councilman Webster was doing an address about Toys on Patrol. It's something he gets behind every year because it helps kids, the community, and law enforcement. That's what the press release said. Officers and deputies carry toys in their vehicles to help comfort kids involved in police interventions. I was getting things ready for the membership drive and the continental breakfast and didn't hear the opening part of the address. But I could hear some of the heckling, so maybe no one got to hear his address. His cousin doesn't need a microphone to be loud, by the way. And I'm pretty sure she gathered homeless folks to be part of the protest. How do you ask them to leave a private event and not be seen as heartless? I had no clue what to do."

"I love the Toys on Patrol fundraiser," Julia said. "I saw a lot of poverty in my years in juvenile court, so I donate a bunch of stuffed animals every year. It's really scary for a child when he or she is in the middle of an accident or an arrest. Hank Webster started Toys on Patrol, didn't he?"

"That's what the notice said. May I have some water, please?"

"Of course." Meredith jumped up. "My bad. Coffee, anyone? I'll get it."

"I'd love some," said Tasha. Julia nodded. Normally they all served themselves, but now that they had Tasha talking, Julia didn't want to stop. A smooth flow of conversation tended to relax the tongue and yield more benefits.

"We used our email lists and social media to get the word out. We deliberately planned the Christmas brunch membership drive simultaneously with the councilman's address because the construction project has wrecked our visitor count. People shy away from paying full price for a scaled-down showing. There was a bigger crowd than we expected. Much bigger. We thought that was great initially."

"It wasn't?"

Tasha shook her head. "We were excited to see local reporters arrive, including two TV news teams, so we were totally high-fiving one another."

"What went wrong?" asked Meredith as she came back into the room with the coffee carafe and mugs on a tray along with a couple of bottles of water.

"The protesters. We realized the press didn't come to hear the councilman. They came to document the protest."

Julia poured herself a cup of coffee. "His cousin deliberately upstaged the toy drive to get her message out. I can't disagree that food for the poor should outrank government-funded Christmas lights, but the toy drive is altruistic too."

"And draws a crowd this time of year," added Meredith. "Kids and toy drives are a big Christmas tradition."

"I think that's why they targeted this event," agreed Tasha. "They started chanting *Empty shelves! Empty shelves! Christmas lights leave empty shelves!*' They had signs and small bullhorns, and they didn't let the councilman speak at all. When he tried to engage them to find out what was wrong, they shouted him down. I called security, but if we tried to clear homeless folks out with cameras running, our public image would be destroyed." She took a sip of coffee. "We staged the event to be totally Christmas themed."

"That makes sense," said Julia.

"Of course we have the annual gingerbread house contest that takes center stage every Advent, and people really knocked themselves out this year. Most of the entries are large and quite beautiful. We put up old-fashioned-looking trees decorated with donated antique ornaments, a gorgeous Nativity scene loaned to us by the Martin & Martin Foundation, and an expertly laid out and decorated continental breakfast catered by Goose Feathers. The buffet was loaded with whoopie pies, cookies, bagels, and croissants, most of which are probably going stale as we speak. The buffet took up the area to the left, and we'd even hired two local college students to serve punch and coffee. I strategically placed the registration table for new and returning members right there so we could make the most of the opportunity to help encourage museum memberships."

Julia looked up from her notepad. "Someone put a lot of thought into this, Tasha."

She breathed deeply. "Me. The events director is out on maternity leave. That was great timing considering this year's lower attendance, so this was my responsibility. And then it all fell apart and we lost a historic display valued at forty thousand dollars."

Meredith choked. Literally. Julia slid a bottle of water her way, and she and Tasha waited while Meredith recovered herself enough to croak out two words, "For bells?"

"Mid-nineteenth-century Scottish handbells," Tasha explained. "A set of forty-three. It's said that these were the bells used by the Swiss Bell Ringers, one of the early traveling acts that P.T. Barnum imported. The campanologists were actually very British," she went on, but Julia stopped her.

"Campana-what?"

"The official name for bell ringers is campanologists," Tasha explained. "It's not a word in common usage anymore. For some reason Barnum thought Swiss bell ringers would be more exotic than British ones, and after their initial resistance, the family agreed because they'd be making significant money here."

"Forty thousand dollars." Meredith sipped her water then her coffee. "For old bells."

"Old bells with an amazing story and sound. But old bells that were also in contention, because the Mulholland family didn't think the museum should have them."

Julia was jotting notes. She paused. "You said they objected to the church's donation, but I don't get it, Tasha. Why did the church have the bells?"

"That goes back nearly fifty years," said Tasha. "Sometime back in the late 1970s Rose Mulholland was tired of the family bickering. According to her granddaughter Emmie, most of the family wasn't bothering with church anymore. They were quite successful at making money, but some marriages were falling apart, there was infighting among the cousins and even siblings, so she took the whole set of bells—three cases, mind you—to her pastor and donated them so that St. Kieran's could have a handbell choir."

"The Mulhollands and the Moynihans were instrumental in getting that parish going," said Meredith. "They were some of the original parishioners and big church supporters."

"And Grandma Rosie was still a parishioner there at the time," said Tasha. "They started a handbell choir that played for over twenty-five years. Then Reverend Mix retired, and the new rector disbanded the bell choir."

"Why?" asked Julia.

Tasha shrugged and sipped her water. "I don't know if anyone knows why. He donated the bells to the museum a few years later, where they've been ever since. Except that made a whole bunch of Mulhollands mad. Some of them vowed to get them back from the museum. They said they weren't the rector's to give away, but by then the church had possessed them for years. I can't imagine a judge giving them back after all that time. In the end they dropped the very pricey lawsuit against the museum. That was right before I got hired about twelve years back, but there's been grumbling ever since. And now this."

Meredith paused in taking notes. "Can you tell us more about the bells' history?"

"Scottish bells and bell ringing were a big thing in nineteenth-century England. As I said earlier, these bells were originally used by the Lancashire Bell Ringers, who were known to Americans as the Swiss Bell Ringers.

"After touring with Barnum for a few years, they returned to England but sold this set of bells to the Peak family, who formed their own troupe in America. But then the Peaks sold the bells to raise money in lean times, and that's how Brian Mulholland got them after the Civil War. He'd seen a performance when they were with Barnum and was so impressed with their sound that he purchased the bells when they became available. It's said that his wife, Mary Kate Mulholland, enjoyed them also, but at that time there wasn't a big enough congregation at St. Kieran's to form a bell choir. So the bells sat unused in storage in the original Mulholland house. Bell ringing fell out of favor, Mary Kate passed away, and by the time bell ringing had a resurgence in the twentieth century, Brian had passed away and no one gave a thought to the bells except his daughter Bridie."

"Bridie Mulholland was a force to be reckoned with in Savannah and Georgia and the entire nation," noted Julia. "I'm not the history buff that Meredith is, but anyone who knows anything about suffrage and women's rights knows the name Bridget Mulholland is right up there with Susan B. Anthony and Elizabeth Cady Stanton. Any female lawyer should have that name on the tip of her tongue. Those women opened doors for us and often did it at huge personal cost."

"Well, look at you." Meredith grinned and raised her coffee mug in salute. "Well done. And you're right. Bridie Mulholland never stopped trying to make the world a better place for women and girls. She's part of the reason that women were not only let into colleges but advanced studies as well. She set the bar high in a number of areas. Hank Webster is her great-great-grandson, and people say he takes after her. When he talks, people listen."

"Not today." Tasha put her face in her hands and said in a muffled voice, "It was a madhouse. A zoo. And at the height of the madness, with Hank asking the protesters to give him a few minutes and he'd address their concerns, and security trying to get the protesters to go down the stairs, and folks refusing and everyone and their brother had cell phones on, taking videos…"

Julia exchanged a look with Meredith, and Meredith jotted something down. There could be interesting footage on those videos. Important footage.

"That's when the lights went out." Julia felt like she was stating the obvious. The best time to create havoc was often during havoc.

"Exactly." Tasha sighed. "Everyone started screaming. We'd curtained off the construction area the day before. The construction crew had scheduled a late start so the noise of hammers and drills wouldn't compete with the event. Because of that we didn't have their work lights turned on. It was pitch black. Everybody turned on their cell phone lights but that meant they started blinding each other with them, so that just made things worse. Folks were falling and tripping over one another. They were in full panic mode, and I was afraid we were going to end up with an absolute tragedy. Of course they were already hotheaded."

"The protesters, you mean?" Julia asked.

"Everyone," she explained. "The people who were there to support the police-sponsored toy fundraiser were furious that the speech had been upstaged, the protesters thought we cut the lights on purpose to clear the place out, and the museum staff was angry that people used a free event to sabotage our hard work in a very tough year. There wasn't a calm head around. Even mine," she admitted sheepishly. "All I could think of was to get people out front safely. At some point in all the panic, Hank Webster disappeared. I imagine his team took the hint and got him out of there before someone got hurt."

"How long were the lights out?"

"Fifteen to twenty minutes. I'm not sure. Once we got hold of the construction foreman, he hooked up some work lights. That helped. And that's when Jay and I discovered the bells were missing."

"No one heard the case break?" asked Meredith. "I'm familiar with the Settlers of Savannah display, and the bells were in a glass case."

"The case was unlocked."

Julia didn't hide her surprise. "Why?"

Tasha ducked her head. "The councilman wanted to do a photo shoot with his family's bells. They were going to use the pictures in a montage or a video, something like that for his upcoming campaign. He wanted people in the shot, in the background, but he said if we unlocked the case while people were around, they'd be all curious about what was happening and wouldn't act natural. His videographer wanted it to look like he was just there, holding one of the bells and talking about the history of his family and the city." She looked up. "I also thought it was a good idea to unlock it without anyone else around so that people wouldn't know it was unlocked."

"So he knew the case would be unlocked. His videographer knew. You knew. And security knew."

"And anyone who may have happened to see us unlock it as folks were setting up before Councilman Webster started talking. They weren't looking our way, but—" She swallowed hard, and her eyes filled again. "It's certainly possible that we were seen."

"And yet it's highly unlikely that anyone who simply happened to see that had prearranged for the lights to go out, protesters to wreak havoc, bedlam to ensue, and the thief to take advantage of the opportunity to slip away with the bells. How many bells, again?"

"Forty-three. In three velvet-lined cases. And they're not lightweight, they're brass over lead. So it's not like anyone could just tuck them under their arm and walk off with them."

"And get them past all of you, down the stairs, and out the front door."

"Exactly. We were right there the whole time." Tasha's phone buzzed. The moment she read the message, tears started flowing again. "The door to the back elevator was open."

Julia frowned.

Meredith filled her in. She'd been a docent at the museum for years. "The back elevator is the service elevator used to bring big pieces up and down."

"Yes." Tears spilled down Tasha's cheeks. "The door to that area is always locked. It's got a new system in place, but when the electricity went off, the person or persons could have gone right over there and taken the elevator down."

"Without electricity?"

"Fire code says that elevators have to be on a backup system, so that worked. It was the locking system that failed with the electricity gone. It's Murphy's Law, for real."

Julia wasn't so sure. "In my life I've often found that Murphy's law about worst-case scenario is often caused by human design or error. And sometimes intentional error."

They had a lot to discuss, but Tasha looked like she could use a break. "Let's get you home," suggested Julia. "And we'll—"

Tasha's phone interrupted Julia's suggestion. Tasha's jaw slackened as she looked at the screen then answered the call. "Hello."

Her face went pale. Her hands shook. And when she hung up the phone she faced Julia and said softly, "There's been a change in plans. Instead of taking me home, can you drive me to the police station? It appears I'm about to be questioned."

Chapter Three

"QUESTIONING IS A PERFECTLY LOGICAL next step," replied Julia. She kept her voice even, but it wasn't easy. "The way to put a puzzle together is one piece at a time, and that's what detectives are trained to do. We'll drive you over and wait."

"We don't know how long it will take." Tasha's face had been splotchy before. Bouts of emotion had brought a blush to her cheeks and throat, but now she'd washed pale. Too pale. "I can't ask you to do that. I'll call my mother."

"Mothers are wonderful, that's for certain," declared Meredith. "But most aren't schooled in the ways of police questioning."

"Except they won't let us in with her," noted Julia. She finished her coffee, stood, and squared her shoulders. "But that's all right, Tasha. You're smart, strong, and brave. You've handled a rough year with grace and dignity. Not everyone going through a tough divorce can put that on their résumé, and you've aced it. You simply answer their questions calmly and directly."

"I expect they've been questioning all kinds of folks this afternoon," added Meredith.

But when Julia walked Tasha into the West Bryan Street stationhouse, the grim-faced detective assured Julia that wasn't the case.

"You haven't questioned anyone else from the crowd, Detective Lansing?" Julia didn't downplay her frown. "From a crowd of over a hundred, several employees, a construction crew, and per diem helpers staffing the food tables? Ms. Alexander is the only person you've interviewed?"

"We'll take the process where it leads," he replied in a level tone that said nothing and everything. He stepped back to let Tasha precede him.

"Can Judge Foley come with me?"

The detective answered the question with a question. "Do you need representation, Mrs. Alexander?"

"I don't know," she answered. "Maybe I do."

"Exercise all the rights you want to, ma'am. Or need to." He nailed Tasha with a stern, dry look. Julia was pretty sure he practiced that look in a mirror. "We've got all day."

Tasha swallowed hard. It took a minute before she replied. "I don't need anyone. I'm fine answering questions on my own."

"This way."

He led the way down the hall and around a corner.

Julia pressed her lips together then drew a breath.

She rejoined Meredith in her car and folded her arms. "Lansing's got the personality of a dried prune."

"Yes. But he's good at his job. Or used to be, anyway. Ron wasn't friends with him, but he respected him and that says a lot." Meredith didn't put the car into gear yet. She faced Julia. "Where to?"

"We need video."

"The local affiliate just ran a quick teaser on my phone app."

Julia frowned. "I'm going straight to social media. Protesters want to be noticed, right? What better way than to post their videos and opinions online for the whole world to see?"

"You're right. And with the museum closed for the day, we won't be able to talk to anyone there anyway."

"Let's hold off on them until Monday," suggested Julia. "We'll want the construction workers and staff on hand."

"And we can get the names of the servers from Tasha."

"For now let's get online and see what's been posted. Between you, me, and Carmen, we should be able to come up with something useful. Do you think Tasha's all right in there?"

Meredith cringed. "I think she's got the guts, but she's guilt-ridden over the setup and not checking things properly. Having that elevator door unlocked is huge. Why would that door be open? Unless someone deliberately left it open?"

Julia jotted the question in her notebook.

Meredith drove them back to the office. A chilly rain had drifted in, and the temperature was in the low sixties. She parked the car, and the ladies hurried inside through the door facing Howard Street. They slung their damp jackets on the pegs lining the kitchen wall near the backdoor stairs.

Carmen came through to greet them. "You're not going to believe what I found. And, FYI, a pumpkin roll, a box of pralines, and something called Dusty Lemon Bars just arrived, all from members of the historical society. What're we going to do with all of it?" She swept the overflowing counters surrounding the kitchen with a look of concern. "You either have too many friends or too many grateful clients. I don't remember it being like this last year."

"Chase is coming down tonight."

Meredith had two sons, Carter and Chase. Carter lived two hours away in Charleston with his wife and two kids. Chase was ten years younger than Carter and a professor at Emory University near Atlanta.

"He does love homemade treats, but even he couldn't make a dent in all of this."

Julia didn't miss the heightened flush on Carmen's cheeks. Chase had seemed smitten with their hardworking assistant, and if that flush to her cheeks was any indication, Carmen reciprocated the emotion. But that didn't solve the problem of excess baked goods. "Timing is everything," she declared. "We donate all but two to the bake sale first thing in the morning. Problem solved."

Meredith frowned. "Won't people be upset to think we donated their gifts?"

"What they don't know won't hurt 'em. This way we make the church some money. I can't imagine any of your friends objecting to that."

That mollified Meredith. "Well, when you put it that way... But I won't be mentioning this to the ladies at the historical society."

Meredith had been president of the Savannah Historical Society for years. She'd stepped aside from the task after Ron's untimely death but still maintained strong ties to the other officers.

"Let's repackage them," said Julia, and Meredith snapped her fingers.

"That's perfect. We can get some paper plates, divide the goodies, wrap them in plastic wrap, and slap a bow on them."

"But first," said Julia, "let's see what we can find online about the protesters."

Julia and Meredith brought their laptops into the conference room. Carmen used her tablet, and in a matter of seconds she'd sent them links to several social accounts with videos and pictures from the morning's events.

"This is why she's invaluable." Meredith muttered the words, pretending that Carmen couldn't hear. "She's a bluetick coonhound on a trail when you put the internet in her hands."

"Despite the canine comparison, I'm going to take that as a compliment," said Carmen. "At my age, I don't remember a pre-internet time. It's always been there. Besides"—she flashed them a teasing smile—"I have to make it look good. No one wants to be undervalued."

"Mere." Julia raised a hand for attention. "Check the second link. The picture shot from a slightly raised angle. Do you recognize anyone there?"

Meredith opened the link and frowned. "I see some folks who look like they're really down on their luck, some who look quite fashionable, and some who seem downright angry. But no one I know."

Carmen studied the picture too. "Should we recognize anyone?"

"The protester with the big sign that says WASTE NOT WANT NOT?"

Meredith started shaking her head. Then she paused. Eyes wide, she raised her gaze to Julia's. "That's Fiona Diedrich."

"Fiona *Mulholland* Diedrich," Julia added. She didn't downplay the little note of triumph in her tone. "The councilman's news-hungry cousin was the instigator interrupting his speech about easing trauma for children."

"*¿Su familia?*" Carmen sounded amazed. "*Es loco, no?* Who does that? Who goes out of their way to undermine someone's hard work? And a family member? *¡Stupido!*"

"Don't hold back, Carmen," teased Meredith. "Tell us how you truly feel."

Carmen rolled her eyes. "I say too much, I know, but when I took my government class to get my citizenship, it taught me to appreciate freedom."

"Part of that freedom is the right to protest," noted Julia. "The right to free speech."

"An important freedom and distinction," Carmen agreed, "but to mess things up on purpose when someone is trying to help the community isn't what nice people do. Is it?"

"We'll track down Ms. Fiona Diedrich and find out," Julia drawled. "She's the only person I recognize in the pictures except for that fellow over there. He's more visible in the third link." She turned her laptop so that Meredith and Carmen could both see it clearly. "He looks familiar."

"Tony Carlisle." Meredith identified the younger man right away. "Carlisle Security. His dad founded the company thirty some years ago, not long after Ron started Bellefontaine Investigations. Tony was a boy then. I haven't seen him in years, but he's the spitting image of his father. Was he there for museum security? Or the councilman's?"

"Do councilmen travel with security?" wondered Julia aloud as she jotted down the name on her pad. "Carmen, can you look up the addresses for Fiona and this Tony guy?"

"Sure," declared Carmen. "Finding elusive people is one of my specialties." Glancing up, she flashed them a grin. "If you gals ever close up shop, I've got the FBI in my crosshairs."

"They'd be blessed to have you, but don't go putting in applications yet," said Meredith. "You are our asset. Not theirs."

"I second that," agreed Julia. "Carmen, can you check to see if Hank Webster has a schedule posted online or if he's off for the month of December?"

"He's working until Christmas Eve," Carmen announced a few moments later. "But his schedule looks full. I mean, the guy does meetings through lunch, so he's not afraid to hunker down."

"How do we get an appointment with him?"

Carmen shook her head. "You don't on his official calendar, but let me dig deeper. See what I can find."

Julia went back to her office to compile a list of what they knew so far. Meredith was on a call for another case, and Julia was just about to figure out a timeline to corner Hank Webster when Carmen poked her head into Julia's office. "Hank Webster is suffering from some interesting financial difficulties right now. And I mean right now." She handed Julia a printout then slid one across to Meredith when she joined them a moment later. "This is the credit report."

"Oh my."

"Exactly," confirmed Carmen. "What's a rich city councilman doing with all this debt and overdue payments? At first I thought I'd made a mistake, but I cross-checked and it's him, all right. He's married, has three very bright kids, and lives in the old Mulholland house on Harris Street. It's worth over one and a half million, so he's real estate rich and cash poor. But how is that possible?"

"I have no idea." Julia examined the sheets closely. "You're sure this is him?"

"Yes. Most of these accounts are closed, but something went wrong for the councilman in the last few months, because he was fine going into the summer. Now he's not. His oldest daughter is a junior at Emory, and the other two are in a private high school. And the house isn't mortgaged. Why go into deep credit card debt instead of just taking out a short-term mortgage on the house? *Es loco, no*?"

"A question we'll ask him tomorrow when we show up on Harris Street."

"Before the bake sale?"

Julia faced Meredith. "I'm going to call the ladies organizing the parish center and make sure they're covered for the early part of the sale. Beau has already committed to helping, so I can join him there for the afternoon shift. That way I can help with cleanup, and we I can take whatever is left to the homeless shelter. If Hank Webster is working nonstop during the week, catching him on a Saturday morning might be best. Any hobbies for him, Carmen?"

"Coaching," she replied immediately. "He's the assistant coach for his daughter's varsity basketball team, and they've got a tournament this weekend, so he should be easy to find at the Mulholland-Moynihan Fitness Center. Her game schedule is printing right now."

"That's almost too easy."

"Well, Fiona might be tougher to nail down," Meredith said. "She's a rabble-rouser of the highest order and involved in a whole bunch of causes. She seems to have a rage-against-the-machine mindset, but I can't fault her for this latest crusade."

Carmen raised her eyebrows. "Which is?"

"More money for the homeless and the food pantries. Her group is upset that the university's Cooperative Extension got big bucks and used a very generous portion to do the huge Christmas lights display at the Botanical Gardens. Their stance is that Christmas lights are fine, and tons of people put up displays, so did Georgia need to fund one million lights while folks are living under bridges without food or shelter?"

Julia winced. "She makes a good point. I love Christmas displays, but I had no idea that government funds were used for anything like that."

"They use the display to draw attention to the gardens and to raise money. It costs money to make money, it seems."

Meredith turned back to Carmen. "Did you find Tony Carlisle?"

"Carlisle Security." Carmen handed each of them a printed sheet. "Background, staff, and availability. There's no list of clients or client reviews," she went on. "I think they cater to people who prefer ano-nymity and privacy."

"It says that?" Meredith scanned her sheet, frowning.

"I inferred it from the language used on the web page."

"His daddy was and maybe is a bit pretentious, but I expect their methods hold appeal for some folks." Meredith grinned at her.

Carmen tapped a glittered Christmas-red nail to the paper in question. "On that note I'm going to finish up and head home. Clouds this thick should not be allowed in December. The days are already too short. Clouds should be outlawed until at least late January. Give us the extra hour of daylight."

Julia's phone buzzed a text. She scanned it quickly. "Tasha's mother has picked her up and is taking her home. Says she'll call tomorrow. That gives us time to check out the councilman at his daughter's game at the fitness center." She looked up. "That's part of St. Michael's School, right?"

Meredith confirmed that with a nod. "The game is at nine, so if we arrive by eight thirty, we should be there for warm-ups. Chase played varsity basketball, and St. Michael's was a fierce competitor. They beat us in the playoffs and went to the state championships his senior year. They take their sports very seriously."

"I love a competitive spirit," Julia declared. "If we get there that early, that'll give us time to talk with him and then track down Fiona at her home. I'm going to text her to say we're interested in her position on the Christmas lights. That should get us a foot in the door."

"Until she discovers that you're just snooping around." Carmen winked and left the room to gather her things.

"It seems a certain young lady becomes quite animated when a certain young man comes to town," Julia said softly.

Meredith smiled. "And have you noticed he's coming more than once a month now, on a regular basis? You are aware, right, that if something lasting develops, we're at a major crossroads. Either he comes down here to work or she goes up there. That would leave you and me in the market for a new assistant, and our gal would be mighty hard to replace."

"A bridge we'll cross when we get to it," said Julia sensibly. "In the meantime, I'll see you in the morning. All right?"

"Do you want to meet there, or should I pick you up?"

"Parking's a bear by St. Michael's so why don't you pick me up? Then you can drop me at the church after lunch for my bake sale shift."

"Or I can stay and help, which saves me from an afternoon and evening alone."

"I thought you and Quin were doing something tomorrow afternoon." Julia closed her laptop and slid it into her bag. "Wasn't that the plan?"

Meredith raised her phone. She didn't look happy. "Plans change, it seems. He just texted that something came up, so I'm free for the afternoon. And that's fine." She stressed the last word just enough for Julia to know it wasn't all that fine. "I'm content with my life. He's all right with his. And it wasn't like a date or anything."

"Although it would be all right if it were a date," mused Julia as she slung the bag onto her arm. "And it's also okay if it's not."

"See you in the morning." Meredith walked out of the conference room and called down the hallway, "Good night, Carmen."

Carmen waved from the front.

Meredith moved on ahead.

Usually she'd wait and walk out with Julia.

Not tonight.

She wasn't stooped, but her shoulders weren't squared up like usual. She'd had a happy marriage. A great husband. Losing him had been a crushing blow, but Meredith's faith and tenacity helped her muster through. And the one thing Julia knew about Meredith

Bellefontaine: she wasn't the type who ran hot and cold. When she loved, she loved completely, and if Quin Crowley wasn't seeing that as his endgame, he might want to call it a day.

Julia liked Quin. He was a good guy.

But her friendship with Meredith spanned nearly five decades, and Julia didn't take that lightly. Friends looked out for one another, and that's exactly what she intended to do.

Chapter Four

Irish men don't cry. Unless they're deep into their drink, and then the floodgates tend to open for some. But Brian Mulholland didn't drink, and he surely didn't cry.

"They don't leave their homeland either. Or turn their backs on their people, letting everything their families worked for go to ruination because of one or two bad years."

Granny's words had seared into his brain.

He loved her. He respected her. He'd do anything for her, but as he surveyed the once lush, verdant fields of his home-land, he understood a basic truth she chose to deny.

Something had gone grievously wrong with the land here. And not just with Mulholland land, but the nation's land and part of Britain too. As much as he despised his aristocratic British counterparts, he understood that whatever was afoot was mystifying them as well. If their excess of education didn't offer a cure or relief, how could he? And Granny herself had been an English lass once. She'd married an Irish weaver she'd met while teaching the women of Limerick how to create the finest lace worn by some of the world's richest people. Lace that was artfully produced by poverty-stricken hands.

And now successive crop failures threatened everything the Mulhollands and Monaghans had built. Granny might be content with watching everything erode around them.

Brian was not.

"Are ye questioning yourself, my love?" Mary Kate slipped up alongside him. She was wearing a traditional hooded robe, woven by Mulholland workers and shaped by Monaghan crafters.

"That shade of emerald brings out the green of your eyes, Mary, m'love. And you know how I feel when I gaze into their depths, don't you, lass?"

She laughed and gave him a gentle jab with her elbow. "Stop your flirting, Husband. It will not work on me, sir. Four lovely children is plenty, with a mother left to raise them, although how I wished for a little girl." She sighed. "But that time is over for us, my love. It must be."

It was.

He'd almost lost her with Michael's birth. He could handle crop failures and a shattered economy. He could make decisions to work around that, albeit difficult ones. He could begin again in a fresh and growing land, but he couldn't live without his Mary Kate. "As I know, darlin'. Are the boys behaving?"

"As well as boys ever do," she retorted. Then she laughed because she loved their sons, four strapping lads who got along some days and fought like baby cats on others. Most,

actually. "I've sent them off to school, but I wanted you to know that I am right beside you in your decision. I know it's hard." *She gazed at what had been a beneficent land to them. They were among the more blessed. Those working in servitude for British landlords had little means to finance an emigration. The Mulholland and Monaghan businesses set a different path for him and his family.*

"Granny won't come."

Mary Kate sighed. "As expected. She is rock solid and just as stubborn, but she has Maureen to watch out for her. Your sister lives in fear and would not think of getting on a ship, whereas I will seize the opportunity at our fingertips for our sons and their sons and those to come after. We have little control here. While some are accustomed to it—"

"Resigned, I'd say."

She shrugged. "Either way, they accept it. This famine has brought us to the crossroads we'd already considered. Sooner than expected, but nothing we haven't discussed, my love. Maureen has no children. She sees no further than her own well-being, and that of your mother. I see the future." *She lifted her gaze to indicate the humble home they shared with the boys.* "We chose not to live big purposely, even though the mill does well. We suspected our future lay across the sea. And now we know that truth."

She was wise beyond her station. She always had been. While other young women ran about, Mary Kate read and studied and practiced the art of lacemaking from an early age after Walker brought lacemakers to the island. Then, instead of holding the knowledge close to her chest as some did, she shared it with others. And when they'd married, she brought a new branch of embellishment and opportunity to Mulholland Woolens in Cork. In a fairly short time she had tempted a crew of Walker's lacemakers to Mulholland's business. With that accomplished, she sought the council of some dear women of the cloth, and they taught her the makings of Youghal lace.

Mary Kate Mulholland wasn't simply his wife.

She'd become his partner, and her farsightedness and appreciation for the new machine age had broadened the family's horizons and deepened their coffers.

"I must get back. I have a final class to teach to the current girls. I will leave them as wise as I can. From that, their industry and ambition will dictate the tenets of their success."

"The sale of the business will be final two weeks hence."

She reached up and feathered a kiss to his cheek. "And I shall make ready our trunks and goods for passage while you arrange for building anew in a new land. But once there, Husband, I will be at your side working and raising our boys. There are many academies there for children of some means but little for those without funding. My goal will be to employ enough people that many children can then attend classes. An industrious and educated populace is a wondrous thing."

"Already she is changing the face of a city she's never seen, in a land that we do not know, but such is the way of my bride." He said it in teasing but knew the truth. His wife didn't just embrace opportunities to help their accounts and

ledgers. She grabbed every chance to open choices and chances for women and children.

An old faith but a new land.

A new city, new country, new business.

They might flourish or flounder, but they'd do it together, and that was the most important thing of all.

Chapter Five

"I LOVE THAT LOCKER ROOM smell," declared Meredith the next morning.

Julia barely avoided plugging her nose as they approached the big gym. She nailed Meredith with a look of disbelief.

"It's nostalgia," Meredith continued. She seemed quite herself this morning. They'd stopped for coffee on the way to the gym, and when Julia prepared to bring her coffee inside, Meredith had stopped her.

"They don't usually allow beverages on the gym floor," she told her. "A stray ball could knock it out of your hands, and then the floor gets sticky and a player could lose a pivot."

Julia set the coffee back into the cup holder. "I have no idea what you just said, but I'll defend to the death your right to say it."

Meredith laughed and led the way inside. A small table staffed by a high school boy stood between them and the gym.

"Hi. Welcome to St. Michael's."

"Well, thank you!" Meredith gave him her best smile as she handed him four dollars. "Two, please."

The boy glanced down at a sign that listed prices:

ADULTS: $2

SENIOR CITIZENS: $1

KIDS UNDER 5: FREE

WHOLE FAMILY: $5.

The boy looked at the sign then raised a grin. "Perfect. Thank you, ladies. You can go right in."

"Don't you have to stamp our hands?" asked Meredith.

The boy shook his head. "I'll remember, ma'am. The two nicest ladies that have come to the game. I'm not likely to forget that."

They moved toward the gym. "That was a nice thing you did there, slipping him the extra money for a donation," Julia said.

"Not nice at all. I hate admitting that I'm classified a senior, and that's Hank Webster's youngest manning the table."

"How do you know that?"

"Did some online checking last night. And their family picture is over there."

Julia looked where Meredith pointed. Sure enough, hanging beneath an engraved sign that read BENEFACTORS, was a picture of Hank Webster and three nice-looking kids, all nearly grown. "That's a current picture," she whispered.

Meredith nodded.

"Which means he's been a recent benefactor?"

Meredith got her drift then. "Overextended? And at the same time giving big bucks to St. Michael's?" She frowned as they moved into the beautiful new gym.

Warm-up drills had basketballs reverberating across both halves of the spacious facility. The St. Michael's team was in white with kelly green font on the front and bold green numbers on the back. The bleachers were on their left. Coaches were all the way across the gym to their right, but there was no one in the way preventing them from crossing the gymnasium, so they did.

"If you act like you belong, folks don't question you," whispered Meredith as she approached the three St. Michael's coaches.

One coach was on the floor with a stopwatch. The other two were comparing notes. They looked up as the ladies approached. The stopwatch coach looked puzzled.

Hank Webster didn't look puzzled. He looked annoyed, which was probably understandable. The guy was just trying to be a good dad, and Julia respected that. But if this was the only way to get his attention—

She kept moving forward. "Councilman, good morning."

Now the other coach looked annoyed too. "Hey, ladies, it's time off right now. When he's in the gym, he's Coach Webster, and we've reminded the press of that numerous times."

"We're not press," said Julia. "We're from Magnolia Investigations, and one of our clients was at the historical museum yesterday when the Mulholland bells went missing." She turned more fully toward Hank Webster. "We know you're probably as shocked as she was, but we're hoping for insight. The kind of insight family might have, since the bells were in your family for over a century."

He grimaced. "They were. I didn't approve of the church's donation to the museum, but I didn't steal the bells, ladies. I'd never even heard the bells played until Grandma donated them to her friends at the church. All I knew was that they were in three heavy cases stuffed in a cluttered attic. My great-grandma left a stuffed owl up there because she couldn't bear to part with it, and I was pretty sure the thing was going to come to life and peck my eyes out, so I hardly ever ventured up the stairs. Still, it had to be a shock to the museum."

"It was, of course." Meredith commiserated with expression and tone. But then she asked a very important question. "Did you know your promotions person asked for the case to be unlocked and left open so that your postspeech photo op would look unstaged?"

His brows shot up. "My people asked for the case to be left open?" Surprise raised his tenor. "I had no idea."

"I know that forty thousand might not seem like a lot of money when one is financially comfortable, but to most of us it's a hefty sum." She stressed the term "financially comfortable" purposely.

The words tweaked his interest. He looked from Meredith to Julia as if sizing them up. Julia handed him her card. "We don't want to mess up the game, Coach, but we'd like to talk to you. Knowing how quickly December weekends fill up, one day early next week is fine. My number's on the card."

They turned and walked away the same way they came, and when a basketball went rogue and nearly smacked Meredith in the head, a tall girl raced their way. "I'm so sorry!" She made a face of contrition. "It ricocheted off another girl's ball. Are you all right?"

It was Bridget Webster looking at them. A lovely girl. Taller than her dad, she had the Mulholland smile and good looks. Julia looked at her then shifted her gaze to the councilman.

He had a lot riding on truth and honesty. Three kids, no mother in the picture, and a dad whose reputation had been golden.

Until now.

Meredith accepted the girl's apology with her typical grace, and when they left the court to head outside, the boy taking money looked surprised. "You're not staying for the game?"

Meredith shook her head. "We're scheduled to help with a bake sale across town, but we hope your team wins."

"Us too, but we've got a great season ahead of us. My sister's the starting power forward and she's already got offers from Kentucky, USC, Vandy, and UMass. But she said she'll never go north. She's SEC all the way."

"That's a power play right there," Meredith told him, and Julia waited until they were outside before she asked for an explanation. Half of what the boy said made no sense to her.

Meredith didn't laugh at her. "Bridget's playing one of the toughest positions, where you get knocked around a lot but have great scoring opportunities," she explained. "And she's been offered scholarships from Kentucky, the University of South Carolina, Vanderbilt, and the University of Massachusetts. All have great basketball programs, but she wants to stay in the Southeastern Conference."

"I've never understood college sports' affinity for acronyms," said Julia as she got into the car. "Always with the initials. But thank you for explaining. Now tell me this: Does that mean a free ride? Or partial scholarship? Those are pricey schools, and her sister's Physician's Assistant program at Emory is a cool hundred and twenty-five grand without housing. That's some serious money, Mere."

"So you think her program is what's put the councilman into so much debt? Wouldn't he have Mulholland money someplace? Because the family is worth a fortune. But maybe none came his way?"

"I don't know," Julia said. Meredith started the car and headed out of the parking lot. "Something has knocked things off-kilter. And where's his wife? She wasn't in the picture on the benefactors' wall. But he's listed as married to Amanda Margaret Fischer."

"FSS," said Meredith then flashed a teasing smile Julia's way. "Fischer Shipping Services."

"Very funny." Julia made a face at her. "Yes, and she should be heiress apparent to the family fortune, she and her sister Francesca, but there's no mention of separation or divorce in the councilman's profile. And yet no wife."

Meredith frowned. "Marriages are tough sometimes. Could she be ill?"

Julia shrugged. "No idea, but you know that despite its size, our city has a healthy grapevine. If something was amiss in one of the historic families, folks would hear of it. Wouldn't they?"

Meredith deepened her frown. "I don't know. Every now and again folks are actually granted privacy. Sometimes when you least expect it. But that could easily change, because this is an election year for the councilman."

An election year.

Julia jotted that down on Hank's information page. Why would a politician with a bright future put an election at risk for a forty-thousand-dollar set of handbells? The risk a felony posed would be far greater than the money gleaned, wouldn't it? Especially with an unmortgaged home. She posed the question to Meredith as they approached the Victorian District, just south of Forsyth Park.

"Desperate times make for desperate choices?" Meredith mused. "I honestly don't know, Julia. It doesn't make a lot of sense. You said Fiona's on Maupas Avenue?"

Julia pointed out the house. "Right here. And will you look at those lights?" She focused her gaze on the decorated house as Meredith pulled up to the curb. "Not what I expected from someone who's taken a big stand against Christmas lights." They got out of the car and started up the sidewalk. The two-and-a-half-story Victorian was decked out with all kinds of lights. The porch posts. The rooflines. And three big inflatables lay flat in the yard. Tucked into the right side of the porch niche, with floodlights pointing their way, stood an outdoor Nativity set done in pale cream.

"This is someone who loves Christmas," said Meredith.

"And dislikes government waste?" asked Julia.

A voice surprised them from behind. "Dislikes overuse of government funds for anything that doesn't have to do with governmental responsibilities or the good of mankind."

Julia and Meredith swung around.

Fiona Diedrich was standing there, with one of the cutest dogs Julia had ever seen. The fluffy midsized fellow was adorable and well-behaved. Julia smiled down at the pooch then put out her hand to Fiona. "Julia Foley."

"Judge Foley." Fiona reached out and shook Julia's hand. "We had some kids from our outreach program come before you about ten years back. I was with the pro bono legal group that represented some of the south side's miscreants. You were fair, and that's all anyone can ask."

Julia didn't remember Fiona, but she remembered the legal team. "Your people did their homework and came prepared. Judges appreciate that."

Fiona turned toward Meredith and lifted her brows in question.

"My partner, Meredith Bellefontaine. We operate Magnolia Investigations."

"The judge has crossed over to the other side." Fiona's brows went even higher. "That's a different sort of retirement."

"I expect you understand quite well," Julia said. She didn't indicate the nicely decorated home. She didn't have to. "For someone who loves the festivities of the holidays, you took a mighty firm stand against Christmas lights yesterday."

"And why do you care?"

"Because a collection of bells worth forty thousand dollars went missing during the melee, and at least half those folks were there because you invited them on social media. Was it because you really care, or was it to hassle your cousin Hank?"

"Both." Fiona said it so cheerfully that neither Julia nor Meredith hid their surprise. "I'm absolutely incensed that we scrape for every single nickel for the food pantries and the city shelter a few blocks up from here, but it's fine to supplement the botanical garden with enough money that they can fund a million lights. And it's not just the cost of the lights, it's the cost of folks to put them up, take them down, and the electricity it takes to light them for thirty-five days. Do you know how many people that would feed?"

"A lot." Meredith's sympathetic tone urged Fiona on.

"Hank isn't a bad man, but he's straitlaced."

Julia would generally say the same about herself, but she listened to Fiona's reasoning with an open mind.

"He's a conformist. He likes to do things the way they've always been done. He'd say it's the right way, but life in politics isn't always reality based, so part of my job is to get him to take off his rose-colored glasses. He still walks a tightrope of decorum, the very same one that got him into trouble with his wife."

Julia frowned. "Usually it's a lack of decorum that leads to upheaval in a marriage."

"She's a thief," said Fiona bluntly. "I told him that a dozen years ago. I said there's something wrong with that woman, something shady about her moves, but she was gorgeous and knew how to draw an audience, and in politics, drawing an audience is a good thing. And I don't mean with ribbon cuttings like my great-grandmother did."

Fiona took a deep breath. "Amanda Webster liked to be seen off the ranch, so to speak. On the town. Having fun. And those yacht pictures that someone 'accidentally' got ahold of eighteen months ago?"

A local person had posted pictures of Hank's wife on a family member's yacht the year before. They weren't risqué, but Amanda had seemingly played for the camera, and that had raised some conservative eyebrows at the time. Julia hadn't paid much attention to the ensuing drama, but it seemed to bother Fiona.

She frowned now, clearly disgusted. "Posed. Purposely. She had her own special way of keeping Hank in the papers, and some folks thought it was a breath of fresh air, that it showed Amanda was a woman with confidence in herself. But the family knew she was hanging him out to dry. Fortunately for him he's become entrenched enough that he was able to keep his council seat, but I don't know if that will work this year. His business. Not mine." She punctuated that explanation with an aggravated sigh then went on in an easier tone.

"It's not that I don't like Hank," she said. "I do. But he sees black and white, I see tweed, and there's a major gap between our viewpoints. Let's just say we don't do holidays at the same house at the same time."

"Fireworks?" asked Julia.

"Yes, and old arguments shouldn't ruin family time for the kids." She shrugged. "I was never able to have kids," she said quietly. "There were no big miracle interventions forty-five years ago, so the kids at the outreach program became mine. I leave my mark in my own way." She straightened her shoulders. "And now I need to get inside and get some flyers made. We're giving them out near the car entrance to the light show. We're trying to get people to realize that what the city is spending on the lights could have increased the shelter's funding by twenty percent. I'm afraid though, that when they're voting next November, everyone will remember the gorgeous Christmas lights display and forget about the shelter. If you ask me it's a sad testament on our times, but no one asks me. Come on, Brandy."

The rust-toned dog had sat quietly the whole time, a marvelous trait, and when Fiona proceeded up her walk, the little dog gave a quick glance over her shoulder. Then she gave Julia a doggie smile, absolutely adorable.

"We never got to ask her about the bells," said Meredith as they walked back to the car.

They hadn't. Did Fiona distract them intentionally, or was it just stream of consciousness talking? Julia didn't know, but she kind of liked Fiona based on that first meeting. "We didn't. Not really. She was more interested in dissing Hank and pushing her agenda than talking about the museum." They got into the car and Meredith pulled away from the curb. "You know how we read people, especially when we first meet them?"

"Yes."

"Fiona's what my mother would call a 'pistol.' She'll do what she needs to do to draw attention to things, but my guess is she's on the level."

"But the shelter needs money," Meredith reminded her. "And food pantry shelves are hurting all around the city. They interviewed someone from a food pantry ministry yesterday on *Savannah Speaks*. Need is up and supplies are down, even from the national food bank. That makes things tough for a lot of folks."

Julia spotted Beau's vehicle as they neared the church a few minutes later. "There's my ride home," she declared as Meredith pulled up to the driveway. The church lot was full, and that was a wonderful feeling. "You can just drop me here, Mere."

"Would you mind if I stay and help?"

Julia turned to her. "Isn't Chase home this weekend?"

"He and Carmen are making cookies with Harmony at my house, and then they're going to look at lights tonight. I'll join them for the lights, but I think I'll leave them to their own devices for the afternoon."

Julia agreed instantly. With Quin a no-show for the afternoon, Meredith wouldn't want to feel like a fifth wheel in her own kitchen.

They parked up the street and walked back to the church. Beau was running the cookie booth, his annual favorite. Julia was never sure if that was because he loved the kids or the cookies. It might have been both.

By the time three o'clock rolled around, they had five dozen cookies, three cakes, two strudel-like things that looked rather dry, and a tray of brownies with nuts left. A preference for no nuts seemed to be a theme of the day.

Beau crossed the room with a big box of plastic wrap. He set it down and wrapped Julia in a hug. "You outdid yourself, darlin'. Pastor says they raised more money this year than the last two years combined." He lowered his head and whispered in her ear, "I didn't tell him that my life might have been easier if I'd just written him a check last week and let it go."

Julia laughed. "Your life would've been easier, but it's nice to see the church come together for a worthy cause."

He kissed her forehead. "After seeing today firsthand, I can't disagree. Where did you say we're taking the leftovers? All but that little container of raspberry jam-filled thumbprints there. I reckon those better go home with us."

She laughed again. "They sure can. The rest is going to the Old City Mission on Bull. Someone mentioned today that funding and donations are down this year."

Beau patted his back pocket. "I've got a couple of emergency use checks in my wallet, Julie-bean. Let's donate a little more than cookies, all right?"

"More than all right." She kissed him and thanked God for him at the same time. As a retired anesthesiologist and a retired judge, they hadn't had serious worries about money in a very long time. Fortunately they'd seen enough of life in their respective positions to know that need existed all around them, and Beau's big heart made him an active donor in multiple ways.

Meredith headed home to see the lights. Julia and Beau dropped off the baked goods and a check. Then Beau used an app to order fried chicken, mashed potatoes, and gravy with a side of okra and beans for curbside pickup.

He grinned at her as he carried the to-go containers back to his truck.

"The perfect end to a long day," she told him, smiling.

"A long couple of weeks," he replied as he nestled the box between them. "Darlin', one of these days you need to figure out what it is about December that puts you in overdrive. Not that I mind being busy with you, but I mind seeing my wife stressed over a time that shouldn't be stressful. It should be peaceful and calm, like Ed talked about last Sunday."

"Pastor Ed has a wife, Beau, and therefore his words of wisdom lose some of their credibility. He has someone else taking care of the details for him."

Beau laughed. "There's more than one grain of truth in that. Naomi keeps things organized. I'm not saying you should slow down." He angled her a look as they pulled up to a red light not far from their home. "But I'm wondering if maybe you should think about what pushes you to fill December every year. There might be times it would be fun to just get in the car and go see the lights, like Meredith's doing tonight. Or take in a movie. See a show downtown. They're doing that Christmas show at the theater on Bull. I'd like to see that if we could."

"No reason we can't." She tried to sound upbeat but failed as he parked the car in the garage.

Beau unlocked the back door off the kitchen and Julia followed him into the house, carrying the box of food.

"Hey."

He settled his arms around her after she set the box down on the kitchen counter. "I didn't mean to upset you, Julia. I guess

I just don't like how hard you've had to work the last two weeks on the sale. Nothing wrong with a fellow looking after his wife, is there?"

She laid her head against his chest and sighed. "No. I don't have a good answer for you, Beau. It's not that I don't know how to say no." She paused a moment, relaxed in the comfort of his arms. "It's that I *need* to say yes, and that's the problem this year. All the other women are mothers, with so many things to do that I feel guilty not picking up the slack. I know I'm not retired, but I've got more time on my hands now than I ever had as a judge, and I feel guilty if I'm not keeping busy. Doing my share."

He kissed her forehead and held her in the shelter of his arms like he'd done for so many years. And then, in true Beau form, he turned totally and wonderfully pragmatic. "We'll figure that out in time. Right now I need to say yes to that chicken. And if we can turn on the TV for the second half of Dawgs football, I'm the happiest man in all of greater Savannah. With my pretty wife,"—he leaned down and kissed her—"fried chicken, and raspberry cookies. Now this is my kind of Saturday night."

Such a good man.

A dear man. And often fairly oblivious to what was going on around him if it didn't include hunting, fishing, golf, or new updates on surgical sedation techniques. Beau might be retired, but he kept up on everything related to his field. Just in case, he said.

So if Beau noticed her uptick in activity enough to comment on it, maybe there was something to it.

Did she feel guilty being retired from the bench, pursuing a new agenda, and living comfortably?

The smell of the chicken and potatoes had her push that thought aside. For tonight she was home with a cozy fire, a great husband, and one of her favorite foods. That not only should be enough. It was enough.

She filled a plate and snuggled down next to Beau to enjoy the game.

Chapter Six

JULIA WAS JUST FINISHING UP her seventh Christmas box donation when the phone rang Sunday afternoon. "Mere. What's up? Has Chase headed back to Atlanta?"

"About an hour ago," Meredith replied. "But I've come up with something I didn't expect. You know how Fiona kind of brushed off the bell topic yesterday?"

"Yes."

"Well, there's a nearly fifteen-year-old article that she did for one of those city-based magazines that's gone under. It's about families and dysfunction, and the topic was aimed at needy families she'd worked with. But listen to what she says: 'I've found that most families are basically dysfunctional. Even the rich ones. There are skeletons everywhere, and power plays too. When I was a teenager my grandmother gave away a valuable set of bells because she got mad at my parents and their siblings for not going to church. As if church attendance was a thing. Ridiculous, right? She said she got tired of having the bells sitting uselessly in the attic because of old sentimental attachments. "Bells should be used!" she said. Trust me, there was nothing sentimental about old bells. Not for me or anyone else, but they were a thing of value and she should have consulted people. Nope. Not her. It was infuriating, but not because of the money.'"

Meredith paused for a long beat. Julia knew that nine times out of ten, it was absolutely about the money, especially when folks claimed it wasn't.

"'It's about a family heirloom and heritage given away. I'd go to that silly little church and grab those bells back myself if I could, but they use them all the time. Unfortunately, they'd notice them missing. And let me tell you, I'm not the only cousin who feels this way.'"

"She said that?" Julia paused with her hands halfway to the oversized shoe box she was filling.

"Her very words. And she was on the list of cousins that threatened a lawsuit against the church for donating the bells to the museum."

"She was at the museum," noted Julia.

"And deliberately put out the word to gather a crowd to disrupt the meeting."

"But what about the power outage? That's a main component that points to an inside job, isn't it? And how would she get the bells out of there? Even with the elevator open, it's not easy to slide three cases of bells over to it. Where does that elevator go anyway?"

"To the basement staging area. Oh, wait." Meredith was quiet for a few seconds.

"Wait for what?"

Excitement pitched Meredith's voice higher. "They changed the big service elevator a few years back. It opens to the ground floor of the museum on one side. They prettied it up on the first floor so it doesn't interfere with the look of the displays. But it opens to the street on the other side. So sure, someone could have parked in the lane, waiting."

"And put the bells into their car and driven off. Are there cameras there?"

"Good question. We'll find out."

"Well, at least we know how someone got them out, most likely," Julia said. "And the only people who knew that Fiona was gathering a crowd deliberately were Fiona herself and the protesters."

"So it's likely her or one of them."

"Well, that's a letdown, because I was ready to believe her yesterday. Who else was on that list for the lawsuit?"

"Fiona's father, William Mulholland. He passed away a few years back. Patrick Whelehan and Kevin Mulholland, another cousin."

"You said that the grandmother gave away the bells because people weren't going to church?" Julia frowned. "Surely there's more to it than that."

"Maybe Grandma was disenchanted with their behaviors," said Meredith. "They went from shirtsleeves to shirtsleeves in three generations. The Mulholland and Moynihan families worked hard for those first generations, but they weren't born rich. Grandma probably resented her children taking the family's hard-earned wealth for granted and squandering it. But what sentimental attachment could her children have to a set of bells meant for a choir? That makes no sense."

"Families can be weird, Mere. We know that. But it is a kind of odd thing to store for over a hundred years, right?"

"Yes, ma'am."

"And people did strange things in the seventies."

Meredith burst out laughing. "Also true. I'm not sure if those other cousins are involved. We can check them out, but I'm hoping

Hank will contact us tomorrow. I've voted for him the last two times, so I don't want him to be the bad guy or see him implicated in some money scandal. I'll see you in the morning, all right?"

"Yes, ma'am."

Julia finished the boxes and packed them in a large tote for tomorrow night's meeting. The calendar hung above the countertop. Just as she set the last box in place, the phone rang again. Her nephew Wyatt's number flashed in the display. She took the call eagerly. "Hey, Wyatt, what's up? How are you guys doing? Mom keeps me updated, but I haven't seen you since Thanksgiving weekend."

"I know, Aunt Julia, and I'm sorry about that. But we've got a couple of things coming up, and I wanted to get them on your calendar."

Julia picked up a pen. "Ready when you are."

"Maddie has a Christmas concert on the thirteenth, and Kennedy's Christmas play is on the eighteenth. And we're planning the annual family Christmas gathering for Christmas Day."

Wyatt and Anna Beth had been hosting the family get-together for the past few years. She'd had mixed emotions passing the torch to the younger couple, but the little girls had more to do in their own house than listen to a bunch of older folks chatting. But the early dates were wrong. All wrong. Both of those dates were already circled on her calendar.

Wyatt read her silence accurately. "You're already booked."

Julia hurried to reassure him. After all, family ranked first. "I'll rearrange things, Wyatt. No worries."

"It's my fault," he told her. "I meant to call when we got the girls' dates and I didn't, and now here I am, calling at the eleventh hour. Anna Beth won't be happy with me, Aunt Julia."

"With good reason," she teased but then got serious again. There was no way she'd miss holiday times with Wyatt and his beautiful family. "I'll work it out, Wyatt. It'll be fine. And I can't wait to see the girls perform. Does Anna Beth need help with anything?"

"She said if you bring those mini cheesecakes she loves, she'll have the happiest Christmas ever. She waits all year for those."

"Consider it done! I look forward to Maddie's concert and Kennedy's play. I love you, kid."

He laughed and sighed, no doubt glad that she wasn't going to get him into trouble with his sweet-natured but very organized wife. "I love you too. See you next week."

She scribbled the dates onto the calendar and scowled. It was full. Too full.

Not just with her volunteer efforts either. Three days straight this week they had evening commitments, not including the box donation gathering on Tuesday evening. She wasn't heading that up, but she was on the committee, and that meant she should attend.

Beau was watching the late afternoon football game with a couple of his fishing buddies. He'd eat there. She'd opted out so she could get the boxes done. The project coordinator would deliver them to the city missions later this week, age-appropriate for kids in need. It was a worthy cause.

Her phone buzzed a text from Tasha. Boys back home. Not happy. I have to go back to work tomorrow. Scared. I don't want people looking at me, thinking I'm guilty. But I can't stay home. I need my job. I need something to go right in a year that's gone all wrong.

Tasha's fears were justified, and her anxieties had just been magnified by the museum event being hijacked by unexpected protesters and the ensuing theft. That didn't look good on anyone's résumé. She called Tasha, who answered quickly. "You didn't have to call me, Julia. I know how busy you are. And I don't mean to dump on you, but my mother is crying in a corner at her house, and I don't know who to talk to."

"Call me anytime," Julia replied. "Stuff like this is hard on mothers because they don't know how to fix it. It's out of their control."

"She asked me if I did it."

Julia's heart went thud. "Did she really?"

"Yes. So if your own mother thinks you're capable of doing something like this, who else thinks that?"

"I have no doubts about you," Julia assured her. Tasha might have had means and motive, but she was honest and forthright. She worked hard to do a good job with her kids and her career, and Julia admired that. "So you call me if things get rough and I'll talk you down, okay? We're in your corner, Tasha."

Tasha breathed a sigh of relief. "Thank you."

"You're welcome. But while I've got you on the phone, we did some social media research and I saw several folks on a protestor's video that look like they might be homeless."

"That's quite possible," Tasha said. "Folks often stop by for a donut or a sandwich when we have a free event. But that day there were more than usual."

Fiona's influence? Maybe. "How can we talk to them?" asked Julia.

"I have no idea. I mean, I see some of them around on occasion, but I don't know if they live under the bridge beneath the Truman or where. There are several homeless gathering spots not too far from the museum, which is always a sad state of affairs."

It was. Julia and Meredith had gotten help with a case from a homeless man the previous year. If they reached out to him, maybe he would recognize someone in the videos Carmen had captured on social media. It was worth a try. "We'll check that out. You get a good night's sleep and show up at work in the morning with your head held high. It's in times like this that I remember the Serenity Prayer because I know there are things I can change and things I can't. We don't hold the reins, God does. And sometimes we just have to give Him room to work."

"Thank you, Julia."

"You are most welcome, and I meant what I said. Call me anytime. We'll keep you posted on how things are going on our end, okay?"

"Yes. Good night."

Julia ended the call. She and Meredith would join forces to check out the homeless camps the next day. The thought that a group of people slipped into the museum for a free pastry and cup of decent coffee was a good reminder that not everyone's life ran smoothly.

The Christmas boxes were neatly arranged in front of her.

They would find homes this holiday season along with other contributions for the kids, but something stirred inside her. A niggling. Was she forgetting something about the case?

The clock chimed eight times.

Beau would be home soon, happy that the Falcons won, especially after a Bulldog win the day before.

A good weekend, all in all.

Right up until a text came through her phone a moment later. A photo of her outdoor manger scene, a gift from Beau's parents over thirty years before. Only, the scene looked woefully bare because Mary and Joseph were missing.

Another text followed. Short and to the point. IF YOU WANT YOUR STATUES BACK, LEAVE THE BELLS ALONE. OR ELSE. Another photo followed. This time of a dumpster, like the kind found all over the Savannah business districts.

The threat was quite clear.

Dump the case or Mary and Joseph would meet an unhappy end in the junkyard.

She stared at the pictures then checked her video doorbell system.

It showed nothing.

How could that be?

Beau came through the back door, elated with the double weekend victories. She met him halfway across the kitchen and held up her phone. "Mary and Joseph have been kidnapped."

He stared at the texts then her. "Julia, someone actually came into our yard and stole the Holy Family? Please tell me this is some kind of really bad joke." He didn't look one bit happy.

"No joke. I wouldn't kid about that beautiful gift from your parents. You know how much I love that set."

Beau went to the window as if to make sure the photo was real. Julia followed and peeked over his shoulder. Sure enough, Mary and Joseph were gone. "I don't like this."

"I don't either, Beau, but I'm not the shrinking violet type either. Someone must want us off this case pretty badly if they're stealing statues."

"My mother picked that set out personally and had it shipped here from New York because she knew you'd love it."

Julia winced. "I know. And she was right. But it kind of makes you wonder, doesn't it?" she asked as she examined the texts once more. "Who steals statues? And why aren't they on our doorbell camera?"

"You checked?"

"Yup. Nothing. That's just weird, isn't it?"

Beau checked the feed too. Then he frowned. "It's not working right. It's offline."

"So did it take a video and we just can't see it?" Julia wondered.

"I'll check it out tomorrow." He frowned. "I have to be honest, with all the deliveries and activity in December, the new system was becoming annoying. I didn't turn it off, but I changed the motion detection settings because we were getting notifications whenever anyone on the cul-de-sac moved."

They'd had the notifications sent to Beau's phone so that Julia wouldn't be interrupted at work.

"I may have messed up the feed, Julia. Sorry. But who would have expected someone to steal things right out of our yard?"

She didn't point out that thwarting theft was the primary reason for installing the techno-savvy doorbell system. "You figure out how we can fix the doorbell tomorrow, and I'll see if Carmen can blow up these pictures. Maybe there's an identifier in there that isn't showing up on the small screen."

Beau tossed his phone on the couch. Julia wasn't sure if he was upset about the doorbell feed or the theft. Probably both.

"I'll fix it, Julia. But the thought that someone has the nerve to invade our space isn't just a concern. It's a worry."

"It's a warning," she corrected him evenly. "It's letting us know that we're making inroads of some kind even if we don't see it. Which means someone's running scared. And that's generally in our favor."

He growled, double-checked the door locks, and stomped off to bed.

He'd be calmer come morning. Beau was a morning person, and he'd get the doorbell and its motion sensitivity figured out with a clearer head then, and she'd leave him to it.

But in the meantime, who had Mary and Joseph, and how far were they willing to go with them?

Chapter Seven

"I CAN'T BELIEVE THEY STOLE the statues right out of your yard. That's galling," declared Meredith on Monday morning. She handed Julia a fresh cup of coffee. The frown on her face matched the disapproval in her voice. "We're not talking Rudolph or a random sheep. It's the Holy Family. No one steals the Holy Family."

"It appears they do," Julia replied as the front door of the office swung open. Their friend Maggie Lu came through the door, looking camera-ready in her red dress, black stockings, and black-and-white tweed winter coat. A black scarf and red gloves almost completed the look, but she was missing the perky black hat she often wore with this coat. "I heard there was a spot of trouble over the weekend, ladies, and I told Rebecca at the library that I'd find out what happened before showing up for my volunteer shift. If I'm not interrupting anything vital, of course."

"Come in," Julia said. "I'd like to use your wisdom on this one, my friend. Coffee?"

"Yes, ma'am, I'd love a cup, and if one of those oatmeal cookies goes along with, I wouldn't say no. I lost my favorite hat to a rogue gusty wind this morning, and there's no saving it, I'm afraid. Off into the street to be crushed beneath the wheels of a passing bus."

"No. Oh, Maggie Lu, I'm so sorry."

"I have others, of course, but saying goodbye to that particular hat is hard."

Julia knew the story behind the hat. "A gift from your son, years ago."

Maggie Lu's eyes grew moist. "He gave it to me right before he was shipped out overseas. It was the last thing he ever gave me." She pulled a tissue from her purse. "I miss him terribly sometimes."

There was a brief silence, then Maggie Lu lifted her chin. "Where shall we talk?" she asked, and the ladies followed her change of subject.

"The cookies are the newest baked goods arrival," Meredith told her as they moved down the hall. "Kitchen or conference room?"

"Kitchen," Julia decided as Carmen plated the cookies. When they'd all taken a seat, Julia explained what had happened from Friday on. When she got to the part about the missing statues, Maggie Lu's brows shot straight up.

"They stole your Nativity? Julia, I can't believe such a thing. It's absolutely unnerving to think they came into your yard, bold as brass, and took those statues away. And no one saw anything?"

"Beau had put our video doorbell into his own personal time-out because it was annoying him with all the December deliveries."

"Oh my word." Maggie Lu's nose wrinkled. "At the worst possible time."

"He's working to redeem himself this morning, and he's going to check with the neighbors, although he doesn't want to cause a panic about thieves. This is clearly targeted at me. Us." She amended the word with a glance around the table. "It's most likely someone trying to make us drop the case. And that's where you come in, Maggie Lu."

Maggie Lu had slipped out of her coat and scarf, but even with the stylish look of her graying hair, it was odd to see her without a hat in winter. "I'll help in any way I can, of course. The Mulholland and Moynihan families have done a great deal for this community since coming here. Their forebearers were hardworking industrialists. Bridget Mulholland wrote that her father's hatred of slavery stemmed from seeing Irish peasants suffer for decades under unfair conditions. This city and this state are blessed to have them, but like so many families in power, they've had their ups and downs."

"Are the two families related, Maggie Lu?" Carmen posed the question, and Maggie Lu nodded.

"The original immigrants were cousins. They came over in the mid-1800s, so the new generations are quite removed. Both families emigrated during the great potato famine. Bridget wrote a bit about her mother's story. It paints an interesting picture of the family, what they left behind and what they brought with them. They had their mill equipment successfully shipped across, so that was a huge accomplishment with so many ships being lost at sea back then. Bridget was a baby when they came across, so she had no actual memories of Ireland, but her parents kept it alive for all the kids. Theirs and the Moynihans. Did you know that Moynihan was spelled differently back then?" she asked, and all three ladies shook their heads.

"The Irish spelling looked like Mon-e-gen to people here. When folks kept mispronouncing it, they changed the name to the spelling they use today. 'Better a new spelling than an old surname maligned.' That was something old Richard used to say, according to Miss Rose."

"You knew her?"

Maggie Lu took a sip of her coffee. She set the cup down as she shook her head. "Not personally, but Miss Rose used to give talks at the libraries and museums back in the day. Sakes alive, that woman could tell a story, and the audiences loved it. She took us back in time and told how the families stood strong on their stance against slavery during the war.

"The Mulholland boys, three of them, anyway, fought for the North and even hired four workers of color when the war was over. One boy stayed home to help run the mill, and that decision got criticized too, but the whole country needed wool."

"Gutsy move," said Julia.

"They were gutsy people," Maggie Lu replied. "Unfortunately this newer generation is a different mix, and I think that grated on Miss Rose. Other than Hank's family, there's been little substance from the current lot. They sold off the mill and the fabric industry for an obscene amount of money about ten years back, and I'm pretty sure most of them aren't busy enough to stay afloat. And that's a sorry testimony to a great family."

"What about the bells she donated, Maggie Lu? The ones that were stolen?"

"You know, she used to tell a story about them, how Mary Kate loved the sound of the bells but for the longest time there weren't enough people in their church to play them. So they sat, unused, and Miss Rose said it was such a shame that the bells should go silent. She donated them while I was teaching, but that wasn't the only thing she gave away." Maggie Lu lifted her coffee cup as Julia posed another question.

"There was more?" she asked.

Maggie Lu set the cup back down. "A lot more. There was grumbling in the family, but Miss Rose knew her own mind and heart. Granny Luv called her 'old cloth,' woven tight and good. But those kids had too much money and turned their back on everything the family had worked so hard to build. It was sometime around then that she donated the bells to St. Kieran's and an array of historical items to the big Irish Memorial in Connecticut. The paper here carried the story and there were some harsh words from her family, but Rose understood heritage. She made sure to keep her grandmother's name alive. She drew attention to Bridget's contributions as a doctor and a suffragist. Those women were workers and givers, and Rose took after them, but the younger ones are a different lot. They've gone soft. All but Hank and his crew, near as I can tell. They're more like the old clan. Working and doing."

Julia exchanged looks with Meredith. "Anything in all of that tweak you?"

"I'm afraid not. Although I wish I'd gone to hear Miss Rose speak when I was young. I expect her take on history was amazing."

Maggie Lu took one last sip of coffee and stood. "She brought it to life," she said as she slipped her coat on. "The good and the bad. And she loved the libraries, so I was able to hear her often, there being no charge when times were tight. A simple bus ride was all it took. And now I must get over to our branch. My shift will be starting soon."

"Take cookies, Maggie Lu." Carmen came back into the kitchen as Maggie Lu prepared to leave. She slid the festive container over.

"We'll keep the ones on the plate, but I have a feeling we'll be seeing more homemade gifts, and you'd be doing us a favor by making these disappear."

"The ladies will love them." Maggie Lu picked up the hand-crocheted black scarf and settled it from shoulder to shoulder. "It's not terribly cold this morning, but there's a wind rising for the afternoon, and I don't like my neck to get cold."

"And it adds a certain panache to the look," noted Meredith with a coy expression, and they all laughed when Maggie Lu smiled.

"One tends to feel good when one looks good, and even better on a thin dime."

"Wise words."

She went out the front as Carmen set a group of pictures down on the table and grabbed a cookie. "This is as big as I can get the photos from the thieves without blurring them. I've circled a couple of things for you to note."

There was a corner of a gold sign behind the dumpster. The fraction they saw was the bottom left-hand corner, but there were lots of signs in Savannah and the surrounding communities. This one had an oldish look to it, the kind of garish yellow that was popular two generations back, but nothing that rang a bell with Julia or Meredith.

The second photo was on grass, and backlit by something. A corner of fencing showed in the blown-up version, a hint that wasn't visible on the phone. "Is that a chain-link fence?" asked Julia.

Meredith peered closer. "It is. And see those two spots there?" She pointed to odd spots in the picture, along the tiny corner of the fence. "They have a dog."

Julia stared closer. "Where?"

"Not in the picture. But some dogs like to dig, and those are a pair of digging spots. Our old dog was famous for that, and it drove Ron crazy because he liked things neat and nice."

"So they have a dog and a fence."

"And the angle of that lighting suggests a backyard," said Carmen. "You don't find too many chain-link fences in front yards, and the lighting is coming from behind and above, so like a back-yard light. On the back of a house."

"And the grass isn't pristine, like you'd find in my neighbor-hood," noted Julia. "I think you're right, Carmen. Were you able to print up pics of the people at the museum? The ones who looked like they might be homeless?"

"Got 'em." She handed them each a set of four pictures. "And if you want to find folks more readily, go by the Liberty Street soup kitchen closer to lunchtime. And take these." Carmen set a cloth grocery bag on the counter. "There are ten blessing bags in there."

Blessing bags were gallon-sized zipper bags that held socks, packs of tuna and chicken, granola bars, and toiletries. "What a good idea."

Carmen nodded. "I keep them on hand. It's not a lot, but it's something. Cold, wet socks are an awful thing."

"These are wonderful, and I'm so glad you do this," Julia said.

"When you gave me a chance to turn myself around, I prom-ised I would never forget how close I came to living life homeless," Carmen told her. "Your help pulled me up. I'm just returning the favor."

"I'm so glad we ran into each other back then." Julia gave Carmen a hug of affection.

Meredith had stepped away. She came back into the room with her coat on. "If we hustle, we can show up at the church door and see what the pastor has to say before we go to the soup kitchen."

"Let's go."

It wasn't a long drive to St. Kieran's. On the way Meredith filled Julia in on what she knew about the historic Irish church that had been built in the early 1860s. "Being Catholic in Savannah was outlawed until after the Revolutionary War, and then that law was revoked in the late eighteenth century. But until the huge wave of potato famine refugees flooded America's shores, there wasn't a real Catholic or Irish presence in the city or the state."

But that was over a hundred-and-sixty years ago. Much had changed since then.

The ladies parked in the church lot. A fellow was working along the edge of the church building, layering a thin seam of grout along a window base.

"Hello?" Meredith called as they moved forward. "We're here to see the pastor. Reverend Martin. Do you know where he might be?"

"He's about the place. I saw him not too long back."

"In the church, you mean?"

"Office, more likely." The man turned to them. "He was here a bit ago, and might be yet, but I didn't see anyone in the office, so I can't say for certain."

"Well, thank you, Mr.—"

"Hopkins," he said. "I keep things up for the reverend. You might want to check the door on the other side. That's nearest his office."

They walked around the front of the old church. They were just shy of the indicated door when a man came out. He looked startled to see them.

"There's no service today," he told them. "I know it said so on the website, but someone forgot to update it, and there is no service. Sorry for your trouble."

He looked sorry. But maybe more sorry for running into them than for having no midday service.

Julia gifted him with her biggest smile. "It's actually you we were looking for, Reverend Martin."

He glanced from one to the other and then his countenance softened noticeably when Meredith took her notebook and pen from her purse. "How can I be of service, ladies?"

Did he think they were reporters or something? Julia seized the moment. "We'd like to ask you about the Mulholland bells."

His jaw dropped and his eyebrows shot up, but he quickly recovered his composure. "A wonderful donation from a marvelous family. When our congregation became too small to use them, the museum was pleased to get them. We were sad that St. Kieran's no longer had the opportunity to enjoy them, but we were glad to have them find a resting place in the community. Especially with the history attached to them."

"Do you mean that they were once part of the P.T. Barnum circus?" asked Julia.

"Yes. After that they were sold to William Peak, who then sold them to the first Mr. Mulholland because his wife had taken a fancy to the bells. Unfortunately she passed away before a bell choir was put into place."

"And that wasn't until the 1970s, right?" Julia continued.

"Sometime in there. Before my time."

"I'm curious as to why you offered the bells to the museum and not back to the family," Julia said. "Or to other churches. Or perhaps you did offer them to the family and they refused?"

"There *are* a lot of them," noted Meredith in a sympathetic tone. "The bells. Not the family. So maybe they didn't want to store them any longer."

The pastor shrugged. "The museum seemed the logical place. They respect history. It seemed wasteful to leave them here, gathering dust. As for giving them to other churches, that would be wrong. I can't unilaterally make a decision like that, and to bring it up to Parish Council would have created a tempest we didn't need as numbers dwindled."

"I've sat on committees and councils, and I know how hard it can be to get agreement." Julia wasn't certain his intent was as altruistic as the man made out. But then, avoiding conflict wasn't a character flaw. "So you didn't need parish approval for the museum donation?"

The pastor glanced at his watch. "I must get on. Good day." He hurried up the two steps and through the church door without another word.

Julia and Meredith exchanged looks. "Interview over?"

Meredith nodded. "So it would seem. But Reverend Martin wasn't very comfortable, was he?"

He wasn't. And as they walked back to the car, Julia wasn't sure if he was uncomfortable with them, the conversation, or life in general. But one thing she was sure of. The good pastor knew more than he was telling.

Chapter Eight

WHEN THEY RETURNED TO THE car, Meredith blew out an exasperated breath. "Something's wrong."

Julia waited.

"With the bells, I mean," she continued. "Twice we've gotten the story that the Mulhollands bought the bells from the Peak family." She typed busily on her phone then sighed. "Mary Kate died in 1872, and the Peak family played bell concerts long before and after that and didn't fall on hard times until the mid-1880s. They were actually housed in a poor house near Syracuse in their old age."

"Does the timing work if the Mulhollands bought them earlier and then the war hit?" asked Julia.

"No." Meredith shook her head. "The Mulhollands didn't come here until the mid-1800s. Would they spend money on a pricey set of bells that languished in an attic for over a century? I can't imagine new immigrants spending hard-earned money on a luxury item that never got used, can you?"

"I'm sure a lot of things went on hold during the Civil War. So maybe." But Meredith had a point. If Brian bought the bells from the Peak family because Mary Kate liked them, why was there no record of them being used? "But if that were the case, it would have been listed in the museum's write-up about the bells, and it's not.

There's no mention that St. Kieran's or any church used them for bell choirs or Christmas hymns until Rose Mulholland donated them over a century later."

"Let's go to the source," announced Meredith. "We're going to find someone related to the Peak family and see when they sold Brian the bells, because maybe this current mystery has roots in a much older one. It may not, but we need to find out."

Julia nodded agreement. When it came to the historical pieces of any puzzle, Meredith's wealth of knowledge and contacts were an absolute bonus. With Savannah's thick history, that affinity was good for business. New news often rested on the shoulders of old newsmakers, and Meredith was the best at ferreting that out.

"I'll put Carmen right on that," she continued. "And we need to speak to the former pastor, the one who was in charge when Grandma Rose donated the bells. If he's still alive and in the area." She took a minute on her phone and then smiled. "He's actually living at Williams Court Apartments over on Lincoln."

"The apartments right across the street from the Georgia Infirmary Day Center, right?" The multistory building held over a hundred apartments geared toward seniors and people in need.

"Yes," Meredith replied. "It seems there are several retired clergy living in the apartments. I read an article in the *Tribune* that talked about Reverend Mix and the euchre club he and some other clergy have formed. They use the day center across the street and have about two dozen people coming to play euchre once a week. Most are former parishioners, and they have sodas, sweet tea, and chips. No buttered popcorn because that messes up the cards."

Julia laughed. "It said that?"

"Sure did. He assured the reporter that folks who love playing cards do not like sticky cards."

"Let's head that way. We've got time before lunch at the soup kitchen. And it's close by."

Julia drove to the apartment complex situated opposite the Georgia Infirmary.

"You want history, it's surrounding us right now," Meredith said as they climbed out of the car. "We're near the site of the first hospital in the country to be dedicated to the health and well-being of aging African Americans, and the training site for some of the first classes of African American nurses. One man's bequest became a corner-stone for healthcare for formerly enslaved people and their families. It was quite different then," Meredith went on. "But it's a blessing that's gone on for nearly two hundred years, and that's saying something."

The went inside the wide lobby and approached the desk. When Julia asked for Reverend Mix, the woman pointed toward the far side of the lobby. "He's right over there with two other gentlemen, and once they've solved the problems of the world, they intend to discuss why we can't seem to get our biscuits to taste like Annie Lovelace's biscuits over there in Nashville, because Reverend Hollister had them several times and there's nothing like them. What's good for Nashville should be attainable on our lunch table, and they're determined to fix it."

"My daddy was the same way," Julia told her. "Once he had time to sit and think, he did way too much of it, God rest his soul, but he did want to help the world. In his own way."

The woman smiled understanding, and Julia and Meredith approached the men.

All three stood as they approached.

Julia appreciated the respect by dipping her chin and smiling. Then she lifted her eyebrows and addressed the group. "Reverend Mix?"

"Oh, it's your turn to be called out, Donnie," laughed one of the men. "I was hopin' it wasn't goin' to be my name she tossed out there, and it wasn't, which means Eddie and I have time to get some fresh coffee and see what's on the afternoon agenda across the way."

Reverend Mix made a face of surprise at the other two men. "You're going to leave me alone to face the onslaught?"

The pair laughed, and one said, "One good thing about being a retired pastor is knowing someone else should be answering life's toughest questions."

Don Mix pretended to frown then motioned for the ladies to sit down. "The two of you don't look all that scary," he said as he retook his seat alongside.

"I would hope we're not," began Meredith. "We just wanted to ask you a few questions about Rose Mulholland."

"Grandma Rose," said the reverend. "A heart for God and the faith of a child. That woman quietly did more for so many than folks will ever know. I know because I was around, and sometimes pointed her in the right direction."

"How so?" asked Julia.

"Folks who fell on hard times. Folks who encountered mental illness. Lost jobs. Divorce or death. Rose was a quiet force to be reckoned with and had the heart of a lion. Hank's like her. He gets things done and isn't looking for credit. But Rose had a spine of steel too, and she ran the family like she was running the lacemaking business before it got bought out by the conglomerate. Not mean. But strong."

"She liked to support the church?"

"The parish and the people in it," he told them. "Her envelope was always there, with an extra one too, to keep the repair budget flush, but she helped in countless quiet ways. Like I said, big heart. And a backbone. Great combination."

"What about the bells, Reverend?"

His expression changed. "I heard they were stolen last week, although what in the name of all that's Southern they were doing in a museum is a mystery to me. They should have been played regularly, such a beautiful thing for a church like St. Kieran's to be blessed with. Oh, the celebrations we had with that choir and those bells." His expression showed appreciation, and his eyes grew misty. "But when the new pastor disbanded Tallie O'Meara's choir, I guess there wasn't really a need. Some clergy love liturgical music. Others find it annoying. I'm afraid I would be at major odds with Reverend Martin on that score."

"Why did Rose give them to the church when they had such a family significance?" Meredith posed the question to him.

He drew his brows together. "I don't recall any special significance that Rose mentioned, and I knew her for well over twenty years as her pastor. She told me they'd been gathering dust in the Harris Street attic for as long as she could remember and said what a shame that was, for bells to never be played. She was quite put out that most of the clan had stopped going to church, and she was bent on making sure some things were taken care of before she passed on. I know she contributed money and Irish artifacts to the big museum they built in Connecticut, and also developed two scholarships at Georgia Southern to supplement her support of their Center for Irish Research and Training. Rose never lost sight of the past and what her ancestors were willing to do for faith, prosperity, and freedom. And of course, being Bridget Mulholland's granddaughter meant the blood of freedom and fairness ran through her veins."

"She kept the Mulholland name when she married."

"She did, and her husband wasn't opposed, because the name meant something. Back then folks weren't using three names or hyphens, so Rose kept her surname and used it to help all she could. Of course, savvy business skills didn't hurt."

"But is it odd that the bells were never used by the Mulhollands themselves?" Meredith frowned in confusion. "Reverend, isn't it a wonder why they had a full set of harmonious bells when no one played them, especially as more and more Catholic churches sprang up in Savannah? It's not the sort of thing one finds in most attics."

He laughed. "I dunno about that. My mother's attic was a frightening spot. It had its share of oddities including headless dress forms that gave me nightmares, so I can't speak to what might or might not be found in attics. You know, there are a couple of old books"—he wagged his finger at Meredith—"the anthology sort, that talk about the Mulhollands, the first immigrants and what they did to build their business and the community. It's old stuff but worth the read. I don't recall the names though. Sorry."

"Don't be, I can check them out. We have an assistant who's good at ferreting out whatever we need. Thank you, Reverend." Meredith stood.

So did Julia. She reached out a hand to him. "Thank you for your help but mostly for your years of service to the community. And I hope you draw a great partner for today's euchre game."

He laughed and shook her hand with a solid grip. "Me too, but if I don't it's still a good game because we get to see folks we wouldn't otherwise. God is good!"

"He surely is." Julia smiled all the way to the parking lot.

As Julia started the car, Meredith pulled out her phone. "I'm going to have Carmen dig up those anthologies. See what she can find out." She sent a text then turned toward Julia. "I hate to dwell on this, but the bell thing bothers me."

"How so?"

"The timeline," continued Meredith. "And the moving. Brian and Mary Kate Mulholland didn't move to Harris Street until she was sick in the 1870s, so that means if they bought the bells—either from the Peaks or someone else—they transported them to the new house and kept them there. Where they stayed, unused for a hundred years despite the rise of bell choirs all over the country in the early twentieth century."

"What if that wasn't the reason?" Julia turned on her directional signal to move into traffic.

Meredith sent her a blank look when they paused at a stop sign. "I don't understand."

"We're accepting that the story we've heard was true," Julia explained. "What if it's not? What if the bells weren't bought for Mary Kate's pleasure?"

"Then why have them?" wondered Meredith. She tapped a finger to her jaw. "You know, that could be something, Julia. I never doubted what we've been told, but maybe you're right. Maybe our mistake is in accepting the story as is. I know folks keep things 'for good.'" She made quote marks with her hands. "My mom did that, and her mom before her, but to me a musical instrument is different. It's not a pretty tablecloth or fine china. It's only useful when played. So maybe you're right. Maybe the bells weren't there for Mary Kate's enjoyment. But if not that, then what?"

It didn't make sense. Would someone who loved the bells keep them sequestered? But then Julia had another thought. "What if it wasn't the bells someone was after?"

Meredith frowned.

Julia went on. "What if it was the cases or something hidden in the cases?"

Meredith's mouth dropped open. Then she closed it and settled back in her seat. "You may be a genius."

Julia grinned. "Well—I don't like to brag." She made a right turn and they drove to the soup kitchen on Liberty Street.

The lunch line outside far exceeded the number of gift bags they had in the car. Julia exchanged looks with Meredith. There were at least thirty-five people already in line for lunch, and there was still a twenty-minute wait until the kitchen opened.

"Let's make more blessing bags and come back tomorrow," Meredith said, and Julia nodded. She couldn't change the world. She knew that. But seeing the noon-hour reality in front of her, she was sure of one thing, and that was that she and Beau could do more.

They made a side trip to the store and returned to the office midafternoon.

Carmen's eyes widened when the ladies carried bags of necessities into the conference room, and by the time they got everything sorted out, Maggie Lu had finished her midday volunteer stint and arrived at the office just in time to help. "I don't know if this will solve a mystery or not, but it will help God's children for certain." She beamed a look of approval around the room and in ninety minutes, they'd filled a hundred bags. Each one held two pairs of socks, easy-open food packs, gift cards to nearby fast-food spots, and a separately wrapped bag of toiletries.

They packed the bags into three boxes and loaded them into Julia's car for the following day. "Now we're ready to ask questions," she announced as she closed the back door of the car.

"And before you gals head out for the night, I just received an interesting answer to a query I put out this afternoon," Carmen told them. "Give me a minute to print it off so you both have a copy."

Meredith turned toward Maggie Lu. "Coffee?"

Maggie Lu declined. "I'm heading to the diner for supper, and I'm about coffee'd out for the day."

"Would you like company?" asked Meredith. "I'm on my own tonight, and if it's not an imposition—"

"Land sakes, it's never an imposition, Meredith!" Maggie Lu exclaimed. "It's an absolute pleasure," she insisted. "I do hate eating alone, and even with my blessed daughter running the restaurant, there's not a minute for her to sit and chat. But eating alone there is preferable to eating alone at home. So yes, let's have dinner together."

Carmen was coming back their way, clutching printed sheets. She handed one to Julia and one to Meredith. As Julia started to read hers, Meredith's phone rang.

She glanced down then frowned and tucked the phone away.

It buzzed a text within seconds, and when she pulled it out, Julia saw Quin's ID on the screen.

Meredith quietly tucked the phone back into her pocket and turned her attention to Carmen. "What did you find out?"

"About the Peak family," Carmen told them. "First off, there are two different spellings of the name, with or without the *e* at the end. Although that's not a big deal. But this is." She held up her phone and read out loud. "'Thank you for your inquiry. Now and again we get questions about the origins of bell ringing in this country, and it seems the Peak family stumbled onto something that was good. At the time it was the next big thing and stood them well for a long time. They did not ever sell their or any bells to a Mr. Mulholland or anyone else in Georgia. There is no record of them ever performing there, although it is known that the Swiss Bell Ringers traveled in that area with Barnum. Is this perhaps the confusion?'"

Meredith exchanged looks with Julia. "That fits in with what we're beginning to think of the timeline. Barnum was performing before the Mulhollands got to America, and their bell ringers returned to London shortly after the Mulhollands would have arrived. The likelihood of them taking in a show while launching a major business and sheep farm seems quite slim, doesn't it? And in such a narrow time frame?"

"Although possible if the circus show was traveling through right then," noted Julia. "Brian and Mary Kate did have several boys, and I expect young boys would love a traveling circus. But again, it's very thin odds that all of that would have lined up and a family of new immigrants would buy something like that. Isn't it?"

"Paper thin," agreed Meredith. "And now we have more evidence that the Peak family didn't sell their bells, so we can be pretty sure that the ones Rose Mulholland had in her attic all those years was a different set."

Julia folded the paper in half and put it in her bag. "Did someone deliberately invent the story about buying the bells from the Peak family to hide something? Or was ascribing the bells to a purchase in the 1800s an innocent mistake, like when a rumor takes on a life of its own?"

"I'll check dates," Carmen promised. "The circus was either here or it wasn't, and it's a narrow enough stretch of time. Then we'll at least know whether it was a plausible story at the time."

Julia's phone buzzed a reminder. "I've gotta go. I've got to meet Beau at six."

Meredith gathered her coat. "We'll see you in the morning, Jules."

"Yes. And enjoy your supper. Give Charlene and the crew my best."

"We will." Maggie Lu's bright smile assured her of that.

As Julia opened her car door the sight of a hundred bags filled with blessings gave her a warm, satisfied feeling. Seeing those filled blessing bags, she knew the afternoon's endeavor really meant something.

Chapter Nine

County Cork, Ireland
April 1847

Shadows lay heavy on fog-filled mornings. Thick fog tricked the eye and could trick the mind if one were given to flights of fancy.

Brian was not given to any such thing, but still—he didn't like the pea-soup fog. It shrouded too much. With trouble afoot and people in need, folks were growing desperate, and desperate people didn't always think clearly.

But Father Seamus O'Shea had asked for a meeting. Nothing unusual about that, but it wasn't a meeting in Brian's upstairs office with a view of the weaving floor. Nor was it in the rector's tiny suite abutting the church.

It was here, by the cemetery that held the priest's family and theirs along with many others.

A shadow moved his way. "Father? Reveal yourself."

"None other. You've come alone, my friend?"

"As instructed but not with comfort in this fog. What's afoot?"

Seamus drew closer then motioned for Brian to follow him to the back side of the small church. "I am in need of a favor. A large one. And I ask it in the name of Holy Ireland, her past and her present."

Brian rolled his eyes, a useless reaction considering the lack of light. "You've uncovered a way to save the homeland and become the independent republic we've longed for? Pray tell, my friend."

"Not the republic but perhaps the reputation of a man of renown. Unfortunately his children care not for the standing of such as us or our fair island."

The good man edged dramatic in his speech and homilies, but he spoke sound doctrine and helped many, so Brian was willing to overlook the theatrical leaning. "Speak straight, Father, for I have much to do. We leave the day after tomorrow, and although my wife is a woman of industry, if I give her no help, she'll be unpacking her rolling pin to thrust me along."

"It is about your leaving. And what you should take."

Brian frowned.

"There is a child, Brian."

Brian deepened the frown.

"A little girl. Very small. Her late mother claimed she arose from a dalliance with a certain middle-aged O'Connell who promised her a life for the child until his wife discovered his excursion."

Brian shook his head in confusion. "Father, I don't—"

"The child's grandfather did much for us, Brian. For you. For me. For the church. He broke barriers that put us into office. He raised the bar high and stood with it."

That O'Connell. *Daniel O'Connell, who served in Parliament and whose sons followed suit.* "Are you saying the child is one of Daniel's grandchildren?"

"*Only to you. But there is talk up north, talk that says the philandering could ruin the standing that Daniel fought so hard to achieve, and there was fear from the serving lady that harm might come to the child if left here.*"

"Shades of Herod, you don't mean it, Father? Someone would harm an innocent child?"

"*Money, power, and greed are wicked taskmasters, and you know what happens when men in power fall away from their faith.*"

Brian knew, all right.

He'd known men of no conscience in his time. He'd bloodied more than an occasional nose because men who bullied their way through life were not to be tolerated.

"Take her, Brian. I will bring her along to the ship and slip her to you with proper payment."

He needed no payment. He was a man of sufficient means. Not wealthy.

Yet.

But he did all right. "We've come so low as to sell children?"

"Never." *The pastor drew himself up. He wasn't a big man, but he was firm in his faith and his teachings, a selfless sort.* "But you're undertaking a great change, and I want there to be no cost to you in this. Can you treat her as your own?"

"I've not said yes, Father."

"Perhaps Mary Kate would be more agreeable?"

"Ach, you don't play fair, despite your station. You know she's longed for a daughter."

"Then maybe the reason God sent four sons was to add this daughter now."

Brian thought a moment but then stopped thinking. "They would actually harm a child, Father?"

"There are some who so desperately want the O'Connell name unsullied as to do whatever it takes. And those few are heartless."

The foolishness of people.

Brian didn't tolerate such in his business or personal life. He'd made strict rules of comportment. Sometimes a man had to thwart the baseness of his nature to be a sound leader. Unfortunately, the opposite was too often true in a quest for power. "We shall take the child. Her name?"

"Bridget."

The exact name his beloved wife had picked for each pregnancy. Four successful and two that were lost.

Bridget Mary Mulholland.

"I will need to arrange passage."

"Done." The priest handed him the necessary papers.

"You were pretty sure of yourself, priest."

"A man of good heart lives true. I will bring her to the boarding area. It will be crowded. No one will know."

But Brian shook his head. "To my home the morning of departure. My new child's safety should be ensured by her father and none other, except the grace of God."

"So be it."

"And now I must go explain this to my wife." The fog had thinned slightly. For a few seconds he saw the pastor's face, and Brian sighed. "You've approached her already."

"If my plea came to naught, hers would weigh well."

Like he said...a man of good doctrine, courage, and insight. "I will see you soon."

The fog didn't begin to lift until Brian was almost home. He came into the house.

The boys were scrambling about outside.

Mary Kate had set bread, butter, and jam onto the table, a feast for a crew of busy boys. He met her gaze.

She met his. And when he gave a slight nod...oh, that smile! A smile he'd fallen for nearly eighteen years before, a smile that made him want to be bigger. Better. Stronger. More faithful, all his days.

She'd soon have the girl she'd longed for. Not of her womb but of her love. And if there was one thing Mary Kate Mulholland knew how to do, it was love.

Chapter Ten

WHEN THEY ARRIVED AT THE Liberty Street kitchen the next morning, the bags weren't exactly an icebreaker, but they were appreciated and that was enough. The workers gave out sixty-seven bags, which left over thirty for the folks that didn't tend to venture out from under the Truman bridge.

After unloading the bags from the car, Julia began showing the museum pictures, starting at the front of the lunch line. "We're looking for information about what happened at the museum last Friday," she announced.

Faces shuttered quickly, like shades being drawn.

"Not to get anyone in trouble," she went on in a warm, easy voice. "But to get our friend out of trouble. If you know any of these folks we've got circled, we'd like to talk to them. Not for long, just to see what they might have noticed that morning."

"I noticed we never got a bite of muffin or a lick of coffee because someone had to go and ruin it all. It was that foolish-talkin' cousin of the councilman, if you ask me," spouted a middle-aged man with a long braid and a full beard. "She likes hearin' herself talk, and she has a lot of words, but if words don't come with actions they are pretty useless around here." He referred to Fiona

Diedrich. "Some talk and do. Some talk and don't. That's where her shoe fits."

"I agree with Duffy," said the woman behind him. "It's way easier to talk the talk than walk the walk."

Julia recognized her from the pictures but didn't push. Yet.

"And the very thought of food going to waste because of what happened was ridiculous. I didn't just go for the pastries either," she continued. "I wanted to hear what Hank Webster had to say. I voted for him and will again, no matter what his wife's been up to."

Julia homed in on her right away because she was a talker. In the whole line of folks waiting for a hot meal on a cold December day, she and the man in front of her were the only two willing to say much. Meredith held out the picture. "This is you over here, isn't it?"

The woman rolled her eyes. "The last thing I want to see is me looking the way I do now, but I don't suppose you care who I was before all of this, do you?"

"I'll listen."

Julia surprised herself with the words. They had work to do, but the woman's words touched a nerve. How sad would it be to have no one to talk to? No one to listen? With a start she realized that Meredith was in that very boat when they reignited her late husband's business. But not anymore.

"You'll sit down with me?" The woman drew her brows together then stuck out her hand. "I'm Neesha," she told them. "Neesha Oberline. And that's my friend Duffy." She nudged the man in front of her.

"I'm happy to meet you, and I'd like to sit with you," Julia said. "We both will." She and Meredith each accepted a bowl of fragrant chicken vegetable soup and a roll. They sat down with the pair and when the woman tested the soup and found it too hot, she set her spoon down and faced Julia and Meredith. "I had a good job for a lot of years."

Julia listened.

"Right over at the harbor, one of the shipping firms that does so much business, and I was good at what I did. Audit control, making sure what came in also went out and cutting losses by careful checking. It was a good life." She paused. She didn't touch her soup or the roll. She sat there with a tired expression and then took a breath. When she did that, Duffy laid a hand atop hers.

"My child died. He was killed by crossfire because he was in the wrong place at the wrong time. I'd warned him to stay out of certain areas where gangs hung out, but my Adam had a heart for old folks and he was bent on helping an old friend get things done around the house. He ran errands for him, played cards with him, and sometimes would just call him to see how he was doing. One night he went over there after school to wash windows. Adam liked clean windows. He never minded helping me with that, but he steered clear of laundry." That memory brought a hint of a smile to her lips. Not her eyes. "Two gangs were having it out for neighborhood control. Three young men died that night."

Julia's heart caught.

She remembered that incident. One of the younger gang members had come through her court while the older ones had been tried in adult criminal court.

"You were on one of the cases, Judge Foley."

Julia winced. "I remember that now. I'm sorry, Neesha."

"Well now, you've got nothing to be sorry about," Neesha said. "Me neither. It's not your fault or mine that these gangs exist. It took me a while to go on after my boy's death, and I took a lot of pills trying to make myself feel better, I lost my job, my house, and my husband, and here I am."

She paused and sipped her coffee. "It's taken six long years, but I finally feel hope for the first time." She took a deep breath. "These days I'm thankful for good friends, hot soup, and dry socks. The Lord knows that my gratitude is true and my mind is clear now. Two good starts."

"I'm glad things are getting better for you," Julia said.

"Geographic circumstances notwithstanding, I'm doing all right." Neesha took a bite of her soup. "There's a bunch of us that look out for one another, steering clear of bad apples. I appreciate you listening, but can I see the pictures? I went to the museum hoping for a nice muffin or Danish, and when the whole protest ruckus began it felt like something was up. Something wasn't right."

Meredith leaned in. "In what way?"

"The councilman seemed nervous. Not his usual self. I've seen him speak a couple of times, and he's got a way of talking so that folks listen, but not that day. And when the shouting began—"

"Coming from his very own and slightly daft cousin," interrupted Duffy.

"Well, he looked around like he was almost scared, which made no sense. Fiona Diedrich is a pain in the neck, but she's not scary. So what was he afraid of? What spooked him?" Neesha shrugged. "Then the lights went out, the screaming started, and people were pushing every which way. I wanted to pass by the table with food on my way out, but it was blocked somehow. I couldn't see anything, so there wasn't much I could do about it."

Julia made up her mind then and there to get Neesha a pack of Danish pastries. "You're sure he looked scared?"

She nodded firmly. "Like I said, I've seen him speak twice before and it wasn't the same on Friday."

Meredith slipped another photo to Neesha's side of the table. "Do either of you know these folks?" she asked, pointing out a pair of men on the opposite side of the group. "Or this woman?"

Duffy nodded. "That's Old Bones and Ty Keehler," he said. "They don't hang out much with others. They like being on their own, but they do like a good feedbag. Though you never see them here midday," he noted. "They've got the corner not far from Forsyth Square—a great spot to pick up some change when the weather's decent. And in December, no matter what the weather."

"I don't know her at all." Neesha pointed to the woman in the picture. The worn coat and somewhat natty hat over a bright red scarf gave her a quaint look, like someone's favorite granny at the market. She was wearing darkened glasses, the kind that change color with the intensity of the light, not unusual on a sunny December day.

She was old. In her early eighties, Julia guessed.

"She might be from someplace near Old City Mission," Duffy said. "She doesn't hang out by the bridge."

"You've given us more information than I dared hope for," Julia told them. "And we're grateful. Neesha, have you ever thought of going back to work now that you're doing better?"

A quick spark of hope made Neesha's eyes light up. Then they dimmed. "Not many places looking for a fiftysomething washup, are there? No, I had my chance and I let it slip away like sand in a bottle. That's on me. I do all right." She reached out and patted Julia's hand. "But I thank you for asking."

The ladies said their goodbyes and left. Once back in the car, Meredith pulled out her notebook and jotted some things down. "I didn't feel right doing this inside," she told Julia. "I felt like we were already invading their space. I didn't want them or anyone else to feel self-conscious, but boy, there was a lot to remember. The main thing being"—she tapped the top picture with the pen—"why was Hank nervous? And why hasn't he called us to talk to us? You'd think—"

Meredith's phone rang then. She looked at it and then held it up to Julia.

Hank Webster's name showed in the display.

Chapter Eleven

MEREDITH ANSWERED THE CALL ON speaker, and when the councilman requested a meeting at their office the next day, she agreed quickly.

When she hung up, she turned to Julia. "I'm glad he made the call."

"Me too, but I think we need to do a little digging before we talk to him."

"Agreed." Meredith called Carmen and asked her to do some more background work on the councilman. After she ended the call she said, "Carmen says that Olive Martus delivered a tunnel of fudge Bundt cake for our helping her earlier this year, and Justine Millrose around the corner brought by a festive-looking pineapple upside-down cake because it's 'the neighborly thing to do.'"

"Oh my word, we cannot eat all this stuff."

"Sugar spreads love," noted Meredith cheerfully. "We can take stuff to both Old City Mission and the soup kitchen."

"Good point. Did Carmen say anything about the sign behind the dumpster in the picture I received?"

"No, but I didn't ask. Want me to call her back?" asked Meredith as Julia pulled up to the curb in front of Fiona's house and parked the car.

"No, we'll check later. Right now I'd like to know why Fiona just happened to choose that time to rally the troops. Amazingly convenient that on the day her cousin is there she sets up a deliberately staged protest and the bells disappear from the intentionally unlocked case."

"You think they're in this together?"

"They're family and they were both there."

"Fighting family," noted Meredith as Julia got out.

"That just makes it easier to rile them up, my friend." Julia smiled at Meredith across the hood of the car. "Let's go kindle a flame or two."

They'd gotten halfway up the walk when Fiona's front door flew open and the storm door was shoved with such force that it ricocheted off the porch wall and bounced back, narrowly missing Fiona's face. The man who'd burst through the door swung back. "I told you to stay out of my business, Fee." His tone was low, but the anger reverberated across the decorated porch. "You've done nothing but make trouble for people for so long that I wonder if you have anything left inside you to just be a nice person. A normal person. Your mother's likely turning over in her grave, weeping for the shame of it. Stay out of my life and away from my children, do you hear me? Or else."

He turned.

Hank Webster. And looking nothing like the hardworking, good-hearted representative he'd always seemed to be.

Julia met his gaze.

He didn't waver. Didn't flinch. He came their way and paused on the sidewalk. "I'll see you two tomorrow as planned."

"Ten o'clock," Meredith confirmed softly. Clearly, she didn't want Fiona overhearing.

He strode off, walked three houses up the road, and climbed into a car.

It wasn't his car. Julia knew that because their research had included pictures of his personal vehicle. This wasn't it. Did he drive someone else's vehicle to Fiona's to keep from being noticed by local press?

Maybe.

The women moved forward quickly.

Fiona went to shut the door. "I've nothing more to say to you. Either of you. Go home."

"Except you might want to address how you deliberately staged a distraction at your cousin's public address and how he arranged to have the bell case unlocked prior to the event so that his team could get a few quick campaign shots of the councilman with his grandmother's bells. Pricey bells that disappeared within minutes of the lights going out." Julia arched one brow. "I can't access your financial records, but it's amazing how much you can discover about a person without breaching privacy laws. People think that a ten-second internet video will disappear from sight, but a simple screenshot at the right moment changes that." Julia paused to let that sink in.

"Your Atlanta shopping spree over Thanksgiving weekend was in the five-figure range," Julia continued. "Since you weren't buying a car, would you like to tell us what's going on? What really happened last Friday? We're good listeners."

"I'm not talking to you or anyone else, and I don't know anything about those stupid bells except that my somewhat simpleminded grandmother should have known better than to give away such an important part of our family heritage." Fiona swiped at her eyes then folded her arms tightly across her chest. Julia was pretty sure Fiona wasn't as overwrought as she was making herself out to be.

Fiona sniffed. "She was wrong to do that. But that doesn't mean I'd stoop to stealing."

Julia trained a hard look at her. "You might. Or you might not. And I expect it *is* hard to lose something so dear to the family."

"My grandmother played those bells for us when we were youngsters," Fiona whispered.

Julia had to draw up all her resolve to maintain a straight face. Pretending commiseration, she stayed silent.

"She'd call us in to supper at the Harris Street house when we were just a band of little children by ringing one of those precious bells. So yes, the bells meant something more than the paltry forty thousand they're valued at. They represented our past. Our family. And now they're gone."

She hiccupped and sniffed some more.

Julia didn't dare look at Meredith, because Fiona had told them plenty.

Those bells hadn't been used to call anyone to supper, and no one had played them for Fiona's generation. Grandma Rose had said as much to the retired pastor. So was Fiona behind the theft to pay for her spending spree? Or was she in cahoots with Hank and they'd just had a falling out?

"You know the old adage about how there's no honor among thieves?" Julia kept her voice matter-of-fact. "I hate to think that you and Hank orchestrated this whole thing, but it's looking more and more like that. Now if you talk to us—"

"When pigs fly."

Julia didn't even blink an eye. "That's fine. The truth has a way of coming out. Your story about Grandma calling all y'all in for supper is sweet, but we have testimony that says it's absolutely untrue. Words straight from your grandma Rose's mouth, and we'll back those up with statements from the other Mulholland and Moynihan cousins. Heaven knows there are plenty of them around. We'll see how many of them remember Rose Mulholland ringing a bell."

Julia had said enough. She turned.

Meredith followed suit. They didn't march back to the car. They strolled, taking their time, letting Fiona's lie sink in. When they got to the car, they stood talking for a few poignant seconds, making it look like they were comparing notes.

Then they climbed into the car.

Let Fiona think what she would. She'd brushed them off on Saturday with her winning air, but Julia had heard about Fiona from a fellow who hadn't seen a lot of good fortune in years. Talk was cheap, and actions spoke louder than words. And Fiona's actions seemed to show that.

Julia paused at the stop sign up the road. "Pick a destination, Mere."

"I want to talk to Tallie O'Meara, the former choir director. Her choir used the bells for a quarter century. She must have some insight, or at least some strong feelings on the subject."

"I'm all for that," Julia said. "Pull up her address, and we'll head that way."

After a couple of minutes Meredith had the address. They were almost there when Carmen's signature ringtone came from Julia's dashboard. The opening notes of "La Cucaracha" filled the car.

Julia hit the answer button on her steering wheel. "Hey. What's up?"

"Red velvet cake with sprigs of fresh holly leaves, which are probably poisonous—the leaves, not the cake because it's from Lydia Cooper, and she's just the sweetest thing—I haven't had time to look it up yet, but I will. We have salted caramel brownies from the Gilroys and a signature jar of whipped honey—"

"Winter white!" Meredith exclaimed. "My favorite. That stays, gals. No matter what else happens, the honey lives at the office. Putting that on an English muffin is the best start to any day. Bless Nikki Williams for bringing it by, because I forgot to order a new jar."

Julia and Carmen both laughed. "So that stays," Julia declared. "Carmen, anything further on the councilman?"

"That's why I'm calling," she said. "I was looking into the financial angle, and you know that creditor sheet I printed up for you just a couple of days ago?"

"Of course."

"Wiped clean. All accounts paid off. Nothing outstanding. That's an impossible feat over a weekend, so what's going on there? What kind of clout do you have to have to make something like that happen in forty-eight hours?"

Meredith's mouth dropped open. She closed it and frowned. "I can't imagine. I mean, we did visit him Saturday morning."

"And intimated we were aware of financial problems," added Julia.

"But no one gets their credit report updated like that," said Meredith. "Carmen, you're sure? Right person? Right accounts?"

"Absolutely certain. I took a screenshot and printed it up for you to see because I couldn't believe it. Do councilmen have this kind of power?"

"Not that I'm aware of, but then what do I know?" Julia said dryly. "We're meeting with him tomorrow, so we'll ask about that. And Carmen, can you just double-check the current chatter and see if there's anything of note on social media about him or the kids? Or his wife, Amanda? Something's out of sync there."

"And yet the kids seem delightful, the two we met," noted Meredith. "And I like the councilman. He's fair, and I love saying that."

"I'll check it out. Julia, you have a message here from a Danielle SanFilippo saying she can't host tonight's Children's Box meeting at the center and wants to know if you could take it over."

"She called the office to make that request? Not my cell phone?"

"Probably hoping to leave a message, which is exactly what happened," murmured Meredith. She said nothing more. She didn't have to.

On the one hand, Julia was going to the meeting anyway, so stepping in wasn't a huge deal. It meant an extra hour or two of coordinating efforts instead of being able to go home at eight o'clock, which was what she'd planned with Beau.

So it wasn't a huge deal, but it felt like one. "I'll call her back."

"I'm free tonight if you want help," offered Carmen.

"I'm not, I'm afraid," said Meredith. "I'm meeting Quin for a holiday supper by the water."

Julia smiled. She wasn't so distracted that she missed the happiness in her friend's voice.

She could accept Carmen's offer.

Or decline stepping into the void left by another team member. "She didn't say why she was begging off?"

"No."

"Thanks, Carmen. I'll figure it out, and if I decide to say yes then I'd love your help. An extra pair of hands organizing which distributor gets which boxes would be great." She disconnected the call.

Meredith put her face in her hands as Julia hung up the call.

Julia scowled at her, only partly in jest. "Stop it. I'm going to be there anyway."

"And you were going to be baking anyway, and donating things anyway, and—" Meredith took a deep breath. "It's not the generosity I question. It's letting folks take advantage of you during a time when it would be nice to sit back and relax or go to a twilight service or visit your mom."

Another stab of guilt hit Julia. She hadn't seen her mom since Thanksgiving.

"I should have Mom come for Saturday supper. You know how she loves a fish fry. But that's when we're going to the holiday supper for Beau's old colleagues at the hospital."

"December's crazy. I know."

"And yet yours isn't."

Meredith shook her head. "It used to be. Between the boys and school and church and family and the historical society and Ron's clients, it seemed like every December filled up to bursting and there was never time to contemplate the manger. I decided to put the brakes on about ten years ago."

"Totally?"

"Yes, ma'am. Anything that wasn't family or faith-related got axed. I still helped with some church fundraisers, but the only other things on the schedule were things to do with my boys, grandkids once they came along, and services. It was like I finally woke up to the whole 'Silent Night' side of Christmas, and I've never looked back."

"How did Ron take that?"

"Hated it at first. But then, he wasn't the one arranging everything, making sure that family things were taken care of. I loved my husband to death, but he tended to minimize the level of work that went into holidays or parties or raising kids. By the second year, though, he was fully on board. And I told him he was welcome to go to his client bashes on his own, but I wanted quiet time."

"I like the sound of quiet time, Mere."

Meredith agreed as Julia pulled off the road, across from the choir director's address. "I realized I was being part of the problem. Not the solution. The minute I changed my behavior, December became something to look forward to. Not dread."

Words to ponder.

Julia knew Meredith was right. She felt it.

But could she make a change this year, in the thick of things? Or would she have to make it her resolution for next year?

She wasn't sure, but one way or another, change was in the air, and it was up to her to make it happen.

She pulled into the driveway once the road was clear.

It was a nice old place. Nothing fancy, but not plain either, and just far enough out of town to have some privacy. Tall trees surrounded the yard. A big yard. Huge, even. There was an old-fashioned oversized garage or carriage house behind the house and a large barn way off to the right. They walked to the front door and rang the bell.

No one answered.

They knocked.

No one came to the door.

"How old is this woman?" whispered Julia.

"Old enough to not want to answer her door to strangers," Meredith whispered back. "According to the internet, she's in her mideighties."

"And still driving?" Julia indicated the oversized sedan in the driveway. "That's one huge car."

"I'll leave her a note," said Meredith. She pulled out her notebook, scribbled a note explaining who they were, and then opened the storm door to tuck it between the doors. "Maybe we can call her and set up an appointment. I don't want to scare her."

"I don't think octogenarians scare as easily as they used to," said Julia as they headed back to the car. "Have you met my mother?"

"I sure have, and she's a corker, that one, but is she the exception or the rule?"

"I think a bit of both these days. And I am going to call her to come over for supper one night soon. I don't want to take her for granted. Just because she's crazy healthy now doesn't mean things couldn't change quickly, and I shouldn't be cavalier about it."

"Agreed. But don't say that in front of her," Meredith warned as she climbed into the passenger seat. "She'll waste no time proving you wrong by taking up skydiving lessons or something."

"You know her well."

Meredith laughed. "Know her and love her. I could use a dose of her gumption. I feel positively feeble compared to B.J. Waverly."

Julia angled her a look of commiseration as she backed the car into a turnaround and headed down the drive. "So do I, Mere. So do I."

Chapter Twelve

More fog. Just as thick, and on a day when they must travel. There was no choice. Ocean-going vessels didn't wait for mere mortals who didn't show up at the docks on time.

The foggy conditions meant a delay on the roads, common enough when one lived in Cork, where nearly a third of the days were born in fog.

Normally this would be of little consequence. Brian had sent their trunks on ahead, the house had been sold with some contents remaining, and he'd shipped several things near and dear to his wife on a separate boat. They would arrive in the New World before their owners, and a family there was taking charge, a branch of the Monaghans.

But today the fog unnerved him.

Is it the fog that concerns you? Or the child? Or those who could mean her harm?

He didn't know, but as his boys clambered into the back of the smaller, quicker wagon, a thread of worry snaked around his neck.

Brian feared little. He never borrowed trouble, but his mother had taught him to trust his intuition. To trust that inner sense. If something feels wrong, Brian Maurice, it's because it is most likely wrong. Trust yourself, lad!

Corinne Mulholland had the sixth sense.

Folks respected it. Some feared it.

Not Brian. He saw her gift as a practical tool that had been passed on to him but in smaller measure. Or maybe just about different things. In any case, the cold thread up his neck meant something, and Brian wasn't about to take chances with his family.

Maybe the child should stay here.

The priest could assign someone else to be her guardian. A man of good conscience couldn't let anything, even a child, pose a threat to his family. Could he?

Think, Brian.

Corinne Mulholland's voice came back to him.

When the babe in the manger lay threatened, did Joseph turn his back on the Son of God, letting Herod's soldiers take him? Did he run back to Nazareth and take up his trade?

No.

He fled to Egypt with his wife and their small child, and there he kept them safe until the time of Herod had passed.

Joseph. A man of compassion and honor.

They'd named their oldest son for the historic carpenter, a man who took on the daunting task of raising God's Son.

Brian stepped to the door and whistled lightly. "Come along, darlin'. We're taking a different route this day. We must hurry."

Mary Kate had been studying the inside of their compact home. Making a memory, he was sure, but his tone drew her attention sharply. She met his gaze and hurried to the wagon and took her seat.

She'd no more than done that when a cloaked figure stole out of the shadows. No horse, no cart, nothing of noise. And when he drew up alongside, he reached up and handed Mary Kate a parcel. "May the Lord of heaven and earth guard your lives and guide your wheels."

Mary Kate clutched the parcel to her chest. "And with you, Father. Thanks for the loaves."

"Good bread for a long journey is essential."

"On this we agree. Take care."

"You as well." The priest sounded quite normal and easygoing. No one would guess he'd just given over the illegitimate child of a member of Parliament.

Brian snapped the reins.

The wagon lurched.

He met the priest's eyes.

He didn't want to think what the priest's fate might be if men in power realized his part in this subterfuge. Prior dustups by both Daniel and his sons had been handled discreetly.

He took the left fork of the coast road. It was longer, but it trailed inland, a sheltered route. He'd be less noticeable, and it was unexpected. For some reason, Brian needed to do the unexpected today. And if it took an hour or two longer, so be it. Today the fog was both friend and foe. It hid danger. But it also hid them. And for that he was grateful.

A peep came from the bundle.

The child, making herself heard.

And then a coo, so soft and sweet that he almost thought he hadn't heard it.

Mary Kate bent low, crooning.

The boys, arguing intently in the back, were oblivious at the moment. The addition of a sister would make them wonder, of course, but being boys he didn't expect the wonder would last long. They knew their mother's longing, so adding an orphaned child to the family would make sense to them.

"You said nothing to your grandmother, Husband?"

"What one doesn't know, one can find little to say about."

"Her outspokenness does well in times. Not so well in other moments."

"I said nothing to her or my sister."

"Good." Approval laced her tone. Mary Kate loved his granny, even with her outspoken ways, or perhaps because of them. And she was the only Mulholland left from that generation, so she was the local matriarch.

But she handled his sister with polite distance and Maureen knew it. His wife wouldn't miss her sister-in-law's snooping and probing. Nor would he. He'd miss Granny fiercely. Her strength had helped build his, and they both loved this land. But she refused to see the current downslide.

He could see nothing else, and if his boys—and now his girl—were to thrive, they needed a land of opportunity.

America.

Georgia. And the manufacturing enterprise he intended to build while they worked with the Monaghan cousins to develop the sheep farms. In an area grown rich with cotton, a smart man hedged his bets with something else. He'd watched one land cave under crop disasters.

The diverse offerings of Mulholland Woolens would be their advantage in the land of cotton. He wasn't afraid to be different.

Today's market feeds you now.

Tomorrow's market feeds you forever.

Granny's words. Her strength. Brought to a new land.

The fog had lifted.

He eased over a final rise. The widespread ports lay before them. The masts of tall ships.

Mary Kate breathed in sharply. "We're here. And we're going."

The child, still tucked like a bundle of bread, cooed softly once more. A new chance for them. A new chance for her. And God love her, the safety others might have denied her.

They found the right slip nearly an hour later, and the name emblazoned on the ship's side spoke for them. FREEDOM.

"Ready, love?"

"I will treasure dry land when it is mine once more, but yes. I am ready. And I will kiss the new ground once we go ashore in America, for as much as I love our island, I will embrace the name of this ship forevermore in a country where freedom of religion and speech and the press is not only

appreciated, it's governed. And that will suit me just fine, Husband."

"Odd that I've never seen your speech curtailed, my love, but nice of you to point it out to me."

She laughed then.

He helped her down, and once they'd boarded with their smaller bags, she waited until they were in the shelter of their little room before she drew the cover back.

Wide-eyed, the child gazed up at them.

Blue eyes. Startlingly blue, like a summer morning sky. Honey-blond hair in curling wisps framed her face, and with the cover lifted, she pushed up for a better view of them while they returned the favor. "Hullo, Bridget," Brian murmured.

Mary Kate beamed. "Ah, you're a winsome lass, you are, and nothing like your brothers. Will that difference stand out, lass? Mark you?"

Twin tiny brows shot up as if the question surprised her, and then she gurgled in answer.

"A talker," Brian noted.

"She is. Or will be when words come."

"Oh darlin', between her heritage and her new mother, words will come. They will have no choice. The question is, what will our darlin' Bridie do with them?"

"Why, she'll change the world, Husband." Mary Kate leaned down and nuzzled the baby's cheek, making her chortle. "She'll do as the good Lord intends. For why else would He put her in our keeping in a new land? You, Miss Bridie

Mulholland, shall seize the day in your own time, darlin' lass. And until that time, we will enjoy gettin' to know ye."

The baby smiled up at them.

Both of them.

Then she gazed around as if taking things in. Not in the usual way of infants.

This was different.

She was different.

And theirs. All theirs. "I'll check the wee rioters outside the door."

"And send them in to meet Miss Bridie. And see to the milk in me bag, Brian. And cloths for changin' and burpin'. If you will."

"Gladly, Wife."

She smiled. He returned the look. And then he went to gather their sons.

Chapter Thirteen

By the time Julia and Carmen left the rec center after organizing the donation boxes that night, Julia was bushed. They'd parked side by side. One of the committee members had taken on the task of delivering the boxes, so once they'd matched the tags with the right neighborhood centers and shelters, they loaded his work van and he drove off, whistling.

"Done." Julia high-fived Carmen. "And it would have been another hour at least if you hadn't come over."

"Slowest people on the planet." Carmen never minced words, but this time she was correct. "Get it in, get it done, move on."

Julia laughed. "That is not the way with a lot of folks around here, my friend. First there is the need to talk things to death. Then—" She broke off her sentence right there and pointed to her car.

There was a sheet of paper beneath her windshield wiper. It was folded in fourths, and when she gently worked it from the wiper, she unfolded it. *"And therefore, never send to know for whom the bell tolls; it tolls for thee."*

"What does that mean?" Carmen stared at the note then Julia.

"It's an old John Donne quote that Hemingway used to title one of his novels."

Carmen's brow drew deeper.

"The tolling bell meant someone died. The quote means that each death has a ripple effect on those around it."

"Or it's a simple death threat done quite poetically." Carmen hugged her arms around herself. "What is so *importante* about those bells that someone would make a death threat over them? I don't get it. They're bells. *Campanas.* Nothing more, and no less. *¡Absurda!*"

Carmen was right.

What was it about the bells that made them life and death to someone?

A shiver snaked its way down Julia's spine.

Was there something hidden in the bells? Something worth more than the forty-thousand price tag? Something worth threatening a life or lives?

"I'll follow you home," declared Carmen. "Don't argue. I won't listen. It's not me they're warning. It's you. First the Holy Family and now your life?"

"Or maybe a reminder that lives matter?"

Carmen snorted. "Yah, yah, yah, whatever. You take the high road, I'll take the low one where the desperados linger." She scowled, but she didn't look at all afraid. Just angry that someone had targeted Julia. "And then I'll see you in the morning."

Arguing would be futile. Julia tucked the note into her bag and drove home. She turned down her street, rounded the cul-de-sac, and stopped the car in the driveway.

Mary and Joseph were back.

Her manger scene was no longer an empty creche with a couple of shepherds standing watch. The Holy Family was right where they belonged. Carmen pulled up alongside her, saw the scene, and huffed a breath. "*Loco.* This is all I can say about this case, mi amiga. *¡Muy loco!*"

"Stealer's remorse?" wondered Julia.

"Or a Trojan horse, with a bomb inside."

"Oh, Carmen." Julia burst out laughing but then realized that maybe it wasn't funny. Maybe—

She moved forward.

"You're going to check it now? At night?"

"You're the one who said their return might be a decoy."

"Which I meant as a warning." Nevertheless, Carmen moved forward with her.

Beau came out of the house. "Who's there?"

"Just me, honey. And Carmen. And Mary and Joseph."

Beau strode forward. "They're back?"

"Safe and sound, so it would seem. No explosives," Julia told him cheerfully.

His face was shadowed, but Julia could imagine his expression. "Well, that's something, I suppose."

"This is weird. That's all I'm saying," said Carmen. Julia recognized the edged note in her voice. "When people behave predictably, it's easy to stay ahead of them. Or track them. But giving back the statues, leaving threatening notes, all in the same night means someone isn't all there."

Carmen narrowed her gaze and hugged Julia. Carmen wasn't a hugger. That meant she was truly concerned.

"Head home, my friend," Julia said, returning her hug. "I'll see you in the morning. Maybe things will seem clearer by then. And maybe we'll have images on the doorbell video now that Beau has readjusted it." She turned expectant eyes toward her husband.

He frowned. "It's not exactly in working order, I'm afraid."

"You broke it."

"Almost instantly. Delicate little suckers. But I can check with the neighbors tomorrow. Maybe they caught something."

Old quotes. Returned statuary. Antique bells.

What were they missing? What thread brought this all together? None she could think of.

She waved goodbye to Carmen and followed Beau into the house.

She'd reexamine things tomorrow. Right now a good night's sleep was in order.

Everything would look better in the morning.

Chapter Fourteen

A HUGE BACKUP ON THE expressway meant nothing looked better the next morning, because Hank Webster was coming to the office and Julia was running ridiculously late.

She'd taken the time to check with neighbors who had surveillance cameras.

One showed nothing. One showed the corner of a silver car and a person—a woman, possibly—getting out, but there wasn't enough of an angle to see if the woman returned Mary and Joseph or was simply making a delivery to a house. The acute angle of the camera only showed a corner of the activity.

The neighbors directly next door to Beau and Julia, who had the most likely feed to show anything, were away, visiting a sick family member in New York. Usually they hired a house sitter, but their regular gal had caught the flu and wasn't available.

"I hate texting them to ask with Millie's mother so sick," Julia told Beau as she packed her water bottle into her bag.

"Hospice now," he told her. "Franklyn messaged me last night. Said Millie's upset about living so far away and missing so much time with her mother."

"So not the time to ask them about the doorbell."

"I'd wait," said Beau. "They're dealing with life and death, Julia. We're not. Mary and Joseph are right where they're supposed to be. In my head, that's a win. But I do not want the bell tolling for my beautiful wife, you hear?" He kissed her and gave her a good long hug. Then he pointed to the calendar. "A free night tonight, Julie-bean. I can't say I'm unhappy about that."

"Me neither." She headed to the office and got caught in the traffic jam before she realized she should have turned off the Truman at East Victory. What should have taken fifteen minutes stretched beyond three-quarters of an hour, and that gave her a lot of time to think. Despite the current theme of bells running through this case, none of the pieces were fitting together. Why did bells that were never played have any meaning for this family? That made no sense. And what might be in those cases? A hundred-and-fifty-year-old secret? A hidden stash that had stayed undiscovered until now? Did the family—or someone in the family—need money? And were they really rich, or had something happened to the Mulholland fortunes and they were in dire straits?

But if that was the case, how had Hank's accounts been restored, and all within forty-eight hours?

Julia wasn't an accountant or an auditor, but Wyatt was. She texted Meredith why she was late and then called Wyatt. "Do you have a minute?" she asked as soon as he answered the phone.

"For my favorite aunt? Always."

His answer made her smile. Quickly she explained what had happened with the councilman's accounts and that they were meeting with him shortly.

"First, what you're telling me about just doesn't happen," he said. "So many of those things take weeks to update. They're quite awful, actually. They're quick to point out credit flaws but not so fast to record payoffs, and settlements and credit scores suffer for it. So if his account is in the clear now, it was most likely done weeks or even a month or two ago and the credit report just caught up with it."

"Over a weekend?" Julia highly doubted that credit agencies were sitting inside on a December weekend, registering payments.

"Computers," he assured her. "Payments or late notices get data-entered by whatever banks, credit companies, loan-holders there are, and then the computer feeds the information through twenty-four-seven. In a country of over three hundred million, that's some significant updating. Most merchandiser credit cards and loans are owned by big banks now, so it's actually easier on the credit reporting. Like one-stop shopping. But it still takes time."

She loved that Wyatt made the whole thing sound logical. "So those payoffs could have been done weeks ago. Not spurred by our visit to his daughter's basketball game."

"Exactly. You're pretty powerful, Aunt Julia." He laughed. "But even you can't get the behind-the-scenes creditors to clear their accounts on a December Saturday."

"I'm glad," she told him. "I'm sitting here, stuck in traffic, and was feeling terrible about what the councilman might have had to do to get that all cleaned up over a weekend."

"And I'm glad to set your mind at ease," he said. "I've got to go. Can't wait to see you guys on Saturday."

"Me too!"

She hung up then called Meredith to fill her in. If Hank got there before Julia arrived, she wanted Meredith to have all the facts. As it was, she got to the office and had just pegged her jacket in the kitchen when the councilman came through the front door.

She slipped into her good shoes, put her damp boots by the kitchen heater, and got to the conference room just as Meredith escorted Hank Webster down the hall.

He looked around the conference room.

Then he scanned the upper levels. *Looking for cameras?*

Or dust, Julia decided.

He motioned toward Julia's office. "Can we talk in there, instead?"

"Less likely to be bugged?" quipped Meredith, and to Julia's surprise, the councilman laughed.

"You can record anything I have to say, but I'd like the press kept out of this. No, it's the windows." He made a face. "I try not to be paranoid, but I also try to be careful."

"Seriously?" Julia frowned. "I'm so sorry to hear you have to worry about that, Councilman."

"Hank, please. You've been a judge, so you understand that unpopular decisions can stir folks up. Most of my constituents are fine, but the risk of a fringe element is always at the back of my mind."

"Did the bell fiasco shake things up?"

He shook his head as he and Meredith took seats in Julia's office while she shut the door. "No. In the whole scheme of things, that's just a blip on the radar. I don't say that to minimize your efforts," he went on. "Our last council vote put things in place that some of the shipping firms didn't like, and because we live in an area where shipping is a major part of the landscape, that makes me and my job vulnerable. We're the largest and fastest growing container port in the country, and the city council just stepped on some pretty wealthy toes. That's why my reelection committee wanted me to get out in front of the coming campaign. The whole bell thing is as much a mystery to me as it is to you. No, the reason I wanted to talk with you is because of my wife."

Julia took her seat gingerly. This wasn't the expected direction of conversation, and from the look on the councilman's face, he wasn't opening up by choice. More like necessity. A part of her wanted to let him off the hook. They weren't trying to pry into his private life.

But then, he'd come to them of his own volition, so there was clearly something on his mind.

"Specifically my wife's mother, Louise Fischer."

Meredith folded her hands. "Go on."

He cleared his throat before saying, "My mother-in-law isn't well."

"I'm sorry to hear that," Julia said.

He shook his head. "It's not a physical thing. It's a mental thing. And atypical, something that came on suddenly about a year ago, out of the blue. No one knows what to do about it. Amanda's been working tirelessly to keep it under wraps because Fischer Shipping is a huge conglomerate now. She's working to have her mother removed from any part of it, but it's tough to declare someone incompetent when they appear quite competent on a semi-regular basis. There's already a hefty estrangement between Amanda and her mother because Louise was sure Amanda could have done better than a fellow who sits on a city council, doing little or nothing. Her words, not mine. Anyway, those money problems that appeared on my credit accounts—"

"Are now wiped clean," Julia said.

He nodded. "A process we began about five weeks ago, and it's finally complete. It was my mother-in-law, opening accounts, forging signatures, and messing us up. She was upset because Amanda interfered with a speech Louise was going to make last summer. A speech about how Jack Fischer was ruining the business, was tanking everything, probably hiding money—"

"Jack Fischer is Amanda's uncle, correct?"

"Yes, her late father's twin brother."

"Was he trying to mess up the business?" asked Meredith. "Wouldn't be the first time a family member went rogue."

Hank shook his head. "Absolutely not. The firm uses Calder and Feldman Accounting Associates for forensic investigations to keep things straight. International trade is a complex industry."

Calder and Feldman was Wyatt's firm, but Julia kept that to herself.

"No, as far as I know the company is fine. My wife stands to inherit a massive amount of money at some point, and we have a few people who think Amanda is trying to remove Louise from power so she can step in. That's why I wanted to see the two of you today. I love my job." He splayed his hands. "We don't need money. Between the two families we're ridiculously rich, and we try to help a lot of causes, a lot of people. But this current situation has messed us up for going on a year now, and it's awkward. And looks odd to outsiders, but it's not, I assure you. Do you remember that old movie about the aliens? The Pod People?"

Julia nodded. "Body Snatchers."

"Well, that's our current situation with Louise, who holds the reins of a mega-billion operation on international trade. Something has gone wrong in her head, and no one can figure out what. She's refusing further tests, my wife has been staying at the mansion because she doesn't dare leave her mother on her own, and I've got three amazing kids who are dealing with normal young adult life. As you can see, the fiasco at the museum pales in comparison to all of that. I wanted to be up-front with you two because your husband"—he turned toward Julia—"was the doctor overseeing the anesthesia on my oldest daughter's brain tumor fifteen years ago. I'll never forget how he came into the room, so confident and sure of himself, knowing how careful he had to be and asking us to trust him and the neurosurgeon to do the job. And they did. She's now a high-performing student in the PA program up at Emory, and you'd never know she had anything wrong. He relieved our minds and hearts that day." He smiled. "Neither one of us ever forgot it."

"He's a great guy," Julia said.

"Yes. He is."

"But what about Fiona?" Meredith pressed. "She's said a lot, and she mentioned something about your wife stealing?"

"Fiona's the Mulholland outlier," he said, shaking his head. "She claims to be a peace-lover, but she enjoys upsetting apple carts, even when there's no legitimate reason to do it. Her mother says she was born in the wrong decade and she'd have fit right into the sixties. Most of us give her a wide berth, but I went to see her because I heard she was spreading rumors about my wife. You're not the only two she's talked to, it seems. Amanda has covered for her mother this past year, and we probably shouldn't have done that. Frankly we're in no-man's-land until this gets figured out or until my mother-in-law does something so drastic that control of the company is threatened." He stood. "You know the worst thing about this?"

Julia and Meredith stood also.

"Louise Fischer is a great lady. An amazing woman. I love her. I admire her. And I hate that whatever has gone wrong is turning her into a caricature of the temperamental rich lady because that's not her. But without her cooperation to do further testing, we're sitting on a keg of dynamite, waiting for it to blow. And then she'll have no choice but to get help. We're helpless, and it's not about the money." This time, Julia believed him. "We have enough of that. It's about watching someone you love slide into an abyss and you're helpless to stop it. And neither Amanda nor I can wrap our heads around that."

Julia put out her hand to shake his. "We'll keep this between us. And thank you for your kind words about Beau. I had no idea that your daughter was one of his patients."

He shook her hand and then Meredith's. When Hank had left, they poured fresh coffee, sat down, and faced each other over Julia's desk. "That was unexpected."

Julia stirred coffee that didn't need stirring. "Yes. And sad. What a tough place to be in. I've never had to deal with anything like that. Diminished capacity. It doesn't run in either family, and I haven't given it much thought, but Louise is only three years older than you and me. How do you convince someone who's losing capacity to get help?"

Meredith's expression reflected Julia's. "I don't know, but I think he was being truthful, don't you?"

"Yes." Julia weighed her response for a few seconds. "Although Fiona seemed genuine on first appearance, so maybe I'm more easily fooled than I thought?"

"Julia Foley? Easily fooled? No." Meredith smiled. "Fiona is well practiced, but you figured it out quickly. And I'm pretty sure Hank's on the up-and-up. I'm going with that unless we find out otherwise, and I don't think we will." Meredith leaned back in her chair and steepled her hands. "You know who hasn't gotten back with me? Tony Carlisle. The junior Carlisle at Carlisle Security, the outfit working the councilman's address on Friday. I've left him two voice messages. I think it's time we pay Carlisle Security a visit and see why young Tony was at the museum. It was either to guard the museum or to guard Hank Weber. I think it's time we found out which."

"Now's as good a time as any." Julia grabbed her purse and her keys. "Let's surprise him."

Chapter Fifteen

CARLISLE SECURITY HAD SET UP shop in a suburban area. Nothing about the tasteful four-story building seemed investigation-related. Retail shops faced both sides of the corner location at street level, offering an inviting shopping experience with an almost small-town feel. Genteel Christmas decorations framed the retail windows and tiny white lights rimmed each light post lining the walkway along the building's exterior. Each vintage-looking post held a vibrant holiday-themed wreath. In a day when some businesses down-played the season, this group seemed invested in a cheerful and inviting display.

Meredith paused once she climbed out of the car. "Tony Sr. wouldn't have bankrolled this, and he owns this building. He bought it a quarter-century ago."

"Perhaps he's had an Ebenezer Scrooge awakening?"

Meredith shrugged. "Highly unlikely, knowing him. I haven't seen him since Ron's funeral."

"Do you think the son has taken over?" Julia asked.

"Don't know." Meredith shrugged. "Big Tony was Ron's age, so retirement age now. He didn't like to hand over the reins to anyone, ever. But that was a long time ago." They walked in and pressed the elevator button for floor two. They didn't have to wait long, because when the elevator opened, there was Tony Carlisle Jr.

"Mr. Carlisle." Meredith stepped forward quickly, blocking his avenue of escape. "Meredith Bellefontaine, from Magnolia Investigations. My husband and I worked with your father a few times over the years."

"Chase's mom."

Meredith seized the familiar connection quickly. "Yes. You and Chase played tennis together on the high school team. He never minded that you were first singles, because you were just plain better."

Tony's face relaxed a little more. "A good man then, and I'm sure a good man now." He started to edge around Meredith. "Must run, ladies. I've got a meeting at one."

"Time is always short in December, isn't it?" Julia kept her voice commiserative but didn't exactly get out of his way. "But if you've got just a moment, we need to ask you about the museum incident. Last Friday."

He frowned. "Ladies, I'm—"

"Were you there on a case?" she went on. "The councilman, perhaps? Who knew the protests were going to have such an effect—"

"Or the lights would suddenly go out like that?" added Meredith.

"And the muddle of confusion—"

"The theft of a pricey museum collection, right then and there, and cell phones recording all kinds of things—"

"Ladies." He shifted his gaze from Meredith to Julia and back. "I'm not at liberty to discuss a case I'm working on, so the bulk of your questions will remain unanswered. I can say that I was just as surprised as everyone else by what occurred, but maybe a little more anticipatory than some. With that being said, I must go."

"We'll walk you out." Meredith trotted toward the door, right beside him. "But if you anticipated something happening, Tony, why didn't you do anything to stop it?"

"Because what I was anticipating had nothing to do with the bells," he said once they were outside. "I was there investigating a relationship issue."

"Ah." Julia nodded. "Not always pleasant, but those pay the bills, don't they?"

He sent her a wry look. "They do. When everything went dark, I did see a suspicious exchange between the couple when someone's phone light caught them. And who better than the museum guard to escort the bells over to a conveniently unlocked elevator?"

"Jay Crawford?" Julia couldn't believe what she was hearing. "You think he took the bells?"

"He was there, his girlfriend's going through a crazy expensive divorce, and I'm sure she needs money. Unlocked doors and blackouts are one of the oldest tricks in the book. I wasn't there to investigate a theft, I was there to check on a romantic entanglement. But if you want my opinion on your jingle bell heist, ladies, I'd be nabbing the man in uniform who just recently got a call up to the Savannah Police Department Academy. Guaranteed they're not going to like the fallout from this. Thanks for stopping by." He crossed to his car, got in, and drove away.

"Tasha and the security guard? Involved?" Julia breathed the words softly. "Meredith, do you think he's right?"

Meredith pointed to the coffee shop. "Let's grab something and take it to the car or the office and discuss this. Tony just opened up a whole new line of questioning in my head and I'm wondering why we didn't see it before. Do you think Tasha could be having a relationship with the Jay Crawford?"

Julia had no idea and said so. "I've never seen her go out with anyone, and her husband rarely takes the boys, so she can't go out much. You heard her say that. And they are separated." Her words floundered along with her confidence in Tasha. "So maybe she is in a new relationship? I honestly don't know, Meredith."

Meredith took it in stride. "We'll ask her. I didn't probe too deeply that first day, because she was so upset. So now we dig deeper. Do we want lunch?"

"No." Julia frowned. "I'm mad at myself for not asking those questions initially. That's twice on this case I've let personal feelings get in the way of doing a good job."

Meredith didn't bring it up again until they'd taken their to-go cups back to the car. "Here's the deal," she said. "It's always tricky with people we know well. Or folks we sympathize with. They touch a different part of us, and that's a good thing. So now we reexamine what Tasha said, and maybe what she didn't say. We can't rule her out, but we can figure out who else might have done this so we can clear her name if she's innocent. And if it turns out she's guilty, that's on her, Jules. Not you. And she did say her own mother asked if she'd done it."

"I found that unbelievable at the time," confessed Julia. She puffed air over her coffee and sighed. "Now I wonder if I should have put more weight on a mother's instincts."

"Mothers aren't always the best judge of their children's characters," Meredith said. "Remember what we went through with the Van Valkens?"

Julia remembered, all right. It had been a wake-up call of the highest order. "I sure do. All right, so mothers don't always know their children best. But I'm still bummed that I didn't delve into the most obvious questions with Tasha, and we don't dare stop by the museum and see her. I don't want to put her job in jeopardy."

"Although I'd like to get a look at this Jay Crawford guy," mused Meredith. "We could stop by and offer her an update on what we do know—"

"Which isn't much." Julia frowned, still disturbed that she'd let personal attachments get in the way of solid fact-finding.

Meredith laughed. "Don't be so hard on yourself. This case isn't even a week old. We've uncovered a lot of items of interest and we've found some dead ends. That's pretty normal. No beating yourself up over being nice. You've been a friend to someone going through a tough time. That's something to be commended. Not criticized. Change of subject."

Julia lifted a brow.

"My date last night."

Julia shifted around in her seat. "Dinner by the water with a really nice man."

"*On* the water," Meredith corrected. "A dinner cruise."

"Romantic." Julia raised her cup and bumped Meredith's gently in a toast. "Here's to romance."

"It was very nice. Really nice," Meredith placed her cup in the cupholder. "And crowded too. The cruise took in all the holiday lights up and down the river. Absolutely gorgeous and very Christmas-friendly."

"It sounds wonderful."

"It was." To Julia's surprise, Meredith blushed. A couple of beats went by before she looked up and said, "You ready to head to the museum?"

Julia knew better than to tease Meredith. She took one last sip of her coffee and returned it to the holder. "Yes, ma'am." She put the car into reverse, backed out of the parking spot, and drove to the museum. She wasn't sure what their meeting would hold, but she wanted to see Tasha in her work environment with unjaded eyes.

And she wanted a good solid look at this Jay Crawford person.

Chapter Sixteen

Savannah, Georgia
September 1847

A sharp whistle from the street made Brian come to the window of their sweltering and soon-to-open manufacturing shop. He pushed it up.

There was no rush of fresh air. The open window didn't help. The heat and humidity smacked him in the face. That was a tough thing to deal with. Folks said he'd get adjusted. Brian wasn't so sure. He leaned out and waved to Blue Collier. "Blue. What's up? Ready to give up life on the docks and come work the mill?"

"All y'all are kind to extend the offer, but once again I've got to say no, Mr. Brian."

Despite repeated attempts, Brian couldn't get Blue to call him simply Brian. "My daddy was a docker and his daddy was a docker," the brown-skinned man called back. "What's born in the blood stays in the blood."

"So much for free will," Brian said wryly. "What's up?"

"Crates for you. Followin' behind but not too far. I came ahead so you'd be aware."

The machine parts he'd sent over two weeks before they'd left Ireland must have finally arrived. Hopefully unbroken. "We're ready and anxious. You walked upriver to tell me? Why not send one of the boys?" Blue was a foreman on the docks. He didn't do minor jobs.

"Felt like a walk is all."

"And Miss Honey Simone is fanning herself on her porch, I expect."

"A glass of sweet tea from a gal named Honey is never a bad thing," admitted Blue. "Your things'll be right along."

"I'm obliged, Blue."

Blue crossed the road and ducked through the hanging oaks. Even the trees seemed weighted by the thick, dense air.

Ireland was humid. Thick fogs rolled over the southern end on a regular basis. Rain fell generously on the front side of the island and less so on the eastern shores.

But the combination of a thermometer pumping into the nineties, no breath of wind, and oppressive humidity made his head ache.

"You'll grow accustomed, Brian." His cousin Jim Monaghan spread a paper roll over a metal table as Blue's figure disappeared from view. It wasn't really a table. They had none of those yet, but it was flat wood spread across even legs, so it was close enough. "I've got the layout you wanted." Jim was ten years older than Brian. He was one of the smart Monaghans. There were three smart ones and then the rest.

That had been Granny's take on her brother's grand-children, and she wasn't far off the mark. Fortunately it was two of those three that Brian would be dealing with.

They went over the plan together. He made a few adjust-ments, but Jim knew machines and he knew wool. The plan made good use of the river water's pull. At one juncture the fall of the river would create energy to drive the wheels and drums. At another point, the discharge of dirty water would flow downstream to the harbor. The more work the natural flow of the water offered, the fewer hours he needed on pay-roll. Jim had found some used equipment. They'd buy new as needed, but Jim and Brian shared one major belief: Use it up. Wear it out. Or keep it running.

The first machines had been installed, a series of carders on the first floor, above the wash vats. They'd hired people. But as Jim tacked his plans to the blank wall on the second floor, Brian posed a question he had to ask. "You went to the farms we'll be working with, eh? Personally?"

Jim nodded. He didn't look up.

"And there's enough of a supply?"

"Not local as yet, but it's no matter. We'll ship down from the North. There's a fair share of sheep being grown there, and it doesn't take too long to come down from Pennsylvania and New York. Your farm will help, but that's some years off."

He'd bought nearly two hundred acres upriver. Not a plantation. He had his own thoughts on those. But a well-stationed farm site with wide-open fields and some woods. Two barns with solid roofs. That bought him time to develop a herd. And he had his first sixty ewes arriving, all bred to Rambouillet rams. A few years down the road, his flock would be a force. "Pennsylvania has sheep?"

The thought surprised him, but he'd only seen the teeming, fetid city of Philadelphia. The smell had sickened Mary Kate and two of the boys. They'd left to come south quickly.

"And these suppliers don't utilize enslaved people, Jim?"

Jim's brows drew down. "I'm taking their word for it. But if we're to get going, we need to—"

"I'll not do it."

Jim swung around. "I know what you're sayin', Brian, I hear ye clear as a bell clangin' on Sunday, but their ways are not our ways."

"Our ways are the only way," Brian said bluntly. "We didna hold with such in Ireland, I'll not overlook the same here. If we pay more, we pay more."

"And go under for what? So that you can sleep well at night? For how many nights, cousin?"

"As many as it takes," Brian replied smoothly. "The time for freedom will come and things will go steady. They'll even out. But I can't face my wife and children and say to them I'm dealing with product from slaveholders. If we have to bring in all Northern-grown fibers, so be it. But I don't care to be sellin' my soul, Jim, and you know that well."

Jim's jaw was tight. Then he relaxed. "There are a few down here that produce without using enslaved people. But if we condemn the ones that do, it could spell trouble for us. We're new here. And not yet in good standing."

"We'll leave the condemnation to others for now. But we can quietly embrace our beliefs and know that good comes of it. Is it wool we're accustomed to?" Wool varied from sheep to sheep, and the best wool came from blending Merino ewes with choice rams. Lower quality fabric came from lower fiber wool.

"Some."

"Then let's deal with those and get word out that we want fleece. Lots of fleece. And that we'll pay top dollar for fine batts."

"Had we thought plainly, we should have settled in the North." There was no missing the wry note of Jim's voice.

"Or be the rabble-rousers the Lord meant us to be and create new opportunities here. For farmers and for children. And now I believe my wife is bringing the boys up to see the progress. They'll be in school soon, but she wants them to understand what's expected of them. And me," he added cheerfully.

A soft "hello" sounded from below as several wagons pulled up to the yard. Jim hurried out to meet them.

Brian swung down the ladder to the carding floor and crossed to the outer area to greet his wife.

The older boys were already clamoring about the opportunity to work. Both were quite certain they'd had enough schooling to last a lifetime. Blue had returned to oversee the unloading.

Mary Kate was less certain about the boys' eagerness to end their education, but Brian liked their initiative. He'd *start them basic, as his father had done with him back home. He motioned toward the wagons. "Joe and Liam, run and give Jim a hand with the crates. You'll likely need a wheel cart to get things up the ramp." The incline led from the carding floor to the second floor.*

"Aye, Da." The two hurried away with no argument, eager to help.

The younger two boys, Alec and Michael, avoided eye contact, clearly hoping they wouldn't be tagged for manual labor.

They were scatterbrains still. He wasn't sure if they'd ever share a calm and rational thought, but if anyone could bring them around, it was Mary Kate Mulholland.

"Head off, you two, but mind the river. I've no time to save ye from drownin' this day." He said it teasingly but with a needed firm note because the younger lads hadn't learned to think first as yet.

They were off in a flash, climbing one of the odd oak trees that peppered the area.

He looped an arm around his pretty wife and kissed her. "What say you, Wife?" He indicated their new mill with a wave of his hand. "It's come along this past week, hasn't it?" He'd had a team paint the windows. The brick building was solid and most of the roof was good, but he and the cousins were laying a new roof on the worn sections the next few days.

"Washtubs are settled below." He moved around the corner and pointed toward the subterranean level. "We've got

the slope to ensure natural drainage into the river once we skim the grease. The boys and I lined the firepits, and the metal tubs are in place. They were dear, for sure, but worth it in the end. And then the cooling tubs, grease skimmers, and the release." The rich golden grease became a fine by-product of production. "We begin next week." He tried to sound assured, but nerves rose within him.

Much rode on this venture. It was asking a lot for three families to eke a living out of one business, but if it was well-run and busy, they could get by then grow. In that growth lay security.

"What say you, Miss Bridie?" Mary Kate lifted the now stocky baby from the pram Jim's sister-in-law had found for them. She'd seemed surprised to see the baby but hadn't said a word, and Brian liked her the better for it. "Do you see your da's new business? A fresh start for all of us," she said as Blue and Jim hauled a crate their way.

"This one's your own," said Blue as he settled the crate near their feet. "Odd but with heft."

Jim leveraged his pry bar and worked the top off quickly. He frowned and stepped back. "Pretty cases."

"But nothing of ours," murmured Mary Kate. The baby in her arms cooed in agreement.

Three fine-tooled leather cases filled the crate. Brian was about to protest that they'd been misdirected but Jim spotted a closed, slim leather pouch. He lifted it toward Brian. "It has your name."

"Meanin' it's yours, sure enough," reckoned Blue.

It couldn't and yet it did. Brian unwound the narrow string closure. Inside were papers. Very important papers. Papers showing the birth of Bridget Mary Mulholland some seven months before. Illegitimate papers for a very legitimate purpose.

He hoisted one case and opened it.

A series of bells filled the case. Similar bells filled each case, and their weight and tone marked them as dear.

A note lay within the third case, written without the haste of that final day, with just enough explanation.

Brian—

Here they are, a down payment as promised, despite your refusal, for one never knows when times may grow hard and harsh. Something put by is always welcome, even as assurance against a claim.

I knew ye would agree, for such a one are ye, sir. A friend of honor. A champion. One who would never let an innocent babe become the target of ill will, no matter what family crest she bears.

I know ye refused payment in kind, but if the sale of these bells brings needed cash during hard times, so be it. They were from a grander church up north but gifted by a man with much to lose and so came to me for the assurance of Bridie's well-being, knowing his claim would be her ruination. And likely her demise.

A new venture in a new land has its own pitfalls. These will help see that all goes well, both with the child and my soul. Her family knows nothing of this. They are of the belief that someone has dispatched her as directed by her uncles. That such is not the case, will never be told to the O'Connells. It is our secret, and only ours, and ever will be. God's peace.

S.

Jim let out a low whistle. "They're quite exquisite," he said. "What use are they?"

"A handbell choir," breathed Mary Kate. "Oh for the day to have a church big enough to have such a delight. And they're meant for us, Husband?"

By default, yes. "So it seems. I'll set them on my wagon and take them home later. From an old friend, wishing us well in a new land."

"A blessing."

Exactly that. But as he loaded the cases onto his wagon, he recognized the timing. He'd put the machine parts aboard the cargo ship two weeks before they'd set sail. Which meant the priest had done the same.

I knew ye would agree.

And he had. He directed his gaze to Mary Kate and the wee one.

The baby lifted her chin. Gazed around. As if she knew this was an auspicious moment. A special time. Those eyes, so blue and so clear, took in the multistory building, and when she turned her baby gaze to his, it was as if she knew something he didn't.

Ridiculous, of course.

And yet it wasn't one bit ridiculous because he knew what she seemed to know, that her coming to America was no accident of timing.

It was the Lord's will. And who could say what would come of it? Of her? Or them?

Just the Lord, and Brian had trusted Him thus far. He was willing to trust Him again.

Chapter Seventeen

MEREDITH LED THE WAY TO the museum offices above the display floors.

To their right, blackout curtains blocked the area under reconstruction.

To their left was the open area, including the area that had housed the Mulholland Bell display. "I'll show you that once we've checked in with Tasha." Meredith kept her tone soft. When they got to Tasha's office, two young women were inside, talking with Tasha and a security guard. Julia couldn't make out Tasha's words, but the door wasn't fully closed, so she could see the girls' reactions.

They both shook their heads, and Tasha gave them each an envelope.

They said thank you—Julia heard that much—then turned to exit the room.

Julia stepped back to let them pass. "Thank you." The foremost girl smiled at Julia. They moved down the hall while Meredith and Julia crossed into Tasha's office.

Tasha came forward. "I didn't expect you ladies. Jay, this is Julia Foley and Meredith Bellefontaine. They run Magnolia Investigations, and they're looking into the theft." She didn't look nervous today. Was it the presence of the good-looking security guard? Or just moving beyond the circumstances of the previous week?

"Jay, hello." Meredith shook the man's hand then turned her attention to Tasha. "We wanted to pop in and tell you that although we haven't sorted all the details as yet, we're significantly narrowing the path." Meredith stressed the adverb. "It's amazing what cell phone footage can pull up these days."

Julia kept her eye on the guard, but he showed little reaction.

"That's so good to hear," breathed Tasha. "Right, Jay?"

"You'd make us very happy if you could solve this," he said. He seemed sincere, but then Julia was doubting her instincts. "I've just gotten a long-awaited call-up to the police academy, and I don't want this to be my legacy after six clean years at the museum. The last thing I wanted was to be in charge during the theft of a local treasure. I'm hoping we get this all cleared up before I report to the academy in a few weeks."

"Congratulations." Julia offered him a smile. "It's not easy to get into the academy."

"It's not," he admitted. "I've been caring for my sick mother, so I couldn't devote the time I needed to it before this. I had to turn down one appointment eighteen months back. Mom went home to Jesus a few months ago," he explained, "and I'm honored to get the opportunity offered to me again." He turned toward Tasha. "You don't mind giving me a ride home today? They said I should have my car back Thursday, as long as the part comes in first thing tomorrow."

"Not at all," she assured him.

"What promised to be two days looks like it's going to take four," he told the ladies. "But at least I've got a car, so I'm not complaining."

Meredith commiserated with him. "My son is at the mercy of others when his car breaks down too. But in a city there are always ride services."

"I'm glad to help, Jay." Tasha waved him off. "I'll meet you downstairs at five, all right?"

"Sounds good. Nice seeing you ladies, and thank you for helping Tasha. And me," he added. "None of us wants a cloud of suspicion around us or the museum."

"So that's Jay Crawford." Julia turned toward Tasha once Jay had left.

"He's a great guy," Tasha said. "He helped me get my boys into scouting. His dad was a leader, and Jay was an Eagle Scout when he was in high school. He always says that the lessons he learned in scouting were the lessons that shaped him to be a good person as an adult. I'm so happy he's getting his chance at the academy, and before his wedding next summer. Another thing he put off because of his mother's health, but now they're moving forward, and she's the nicest gal." She clasped her hands together. "So things are going well?" she asked. "I'm so relieved to hear that. I can't wait until this is over. The girls were just asking me if we'd figured out what happened, and I hated to tell them no, but I was glad to pay them for their time at the event."

"The college gals who helped at the continental breakfast table?"

"Yes."

"I wonder if they saw or noticed anything out of place," said Meredith.

Tasha shrugged. "I don't think so. They were at the table. I can show you the setup, if you like, but their vantage point was obstructed by the gingerbread house contest display. They would have been able to hear Hank Webster but not see him or much of the crowd until it dispersed and came their way. But then once the protesting began, no one heard what Councilman Webster was trying to say. Would you like me to show you now?" Tasha moved to the door. "I've got time, and you're here."

"I'm not as familiar with the museum as Meredith is, so yes," Julia replied. "I'd like that. And it's good to see you looking more like yourself, Tasha." Julia sent her a look of approval. "That makes me happy."

"I realized that if I come into work looking worried and guilty, people are going to assume I'm worried and guilty," Tasha explained. "Once I got over the initial shock, I got down on my knees and told God that I could not handle this alone, not on top of all the crazy divorce stuff swirling around me. I said if I can't change what happened, it's out of my hands and firmly in His."

"You handed it off."

"I did, but I can't tell all y'all how happy I am to know there's progress."

There wasn't much. Not really. But there would be, given a little more time. "Inch by inch, like most investigations," Julia said.

They went down the hall, and Tasha led them toward the front. "Will you be at the neighborhood Christmas bash on Sunday?" She posed the question to Julia as they turned a corner.

Julia stayed noncommittal. "I'm not sure. Beau and I are going in multiple directions the next two weeks, and I'm running low on time."

"The boys don't like it," Tasha confessed. "But it seems rude not to go when the Kestlers are so courteous about throwing the party and inviting everyone on the circle. But two restless boys don't make it a fun time, and I'm the only one on the circle with elementary school-aged kids."

There was nothing for kids to do at the Kestler house. The lack of toys or anything imaginative made it a dull afternoon of adult food and boring conversations. Why would any kid want to go?

"Tasha, I have free passes to the December museum tours out on Tybee Island," said Meredith. "One of my history-loving friends works at their museum, and I have three extra." She opened her purse, reached in, and withdrew the passes. "I can't go, and I've already given the other three away, so why not take the boys? It's fascinating stuff."

"That would be awesome." Tasha hesitated a moment before taking the tickets. "But there must be someone you know better than me who could use these."

"Nonsense," Meredith said. "I bet the boys will love it. Attendance is down in December with holiday things going on, so it's a wonderful experience without the crowds."

"Thank you." Tasha slipped the tickets into a pocket of her museum apron and sighed. "We'll all love it. So here's the area."

Tasha pointed to where the buffet tables had been arranged and then to where Hank Webster had attempted to address the crowd. Then she moved back to the table area and waved her hand forward. "You can see from where the girls were standing, the actual speech event was pretty invisible because the gingerbread house contest display is between here and there."

"They're so much fun," said Julia. "Who would have thought to make a two-foot-high gingerbread castle? The details in these houses amaze me." The popular annual contest entries took up a generous share of the area to their immediate left and stretched out at various heights to allow viewing. "Where were the bells?"

"Down here." Tasha led them back to the Hometown History wing and walked down the middle. Former classrooms flanked the hallway, and each room featured historical glimpses of Savannah, then and now. She paused at an oak-trimmed display case about halfway down. "They were in this case."

"And the back was unlocked?"

She winced. "Yes, and of course in retrospect that was a stupid idea. Fortunately the director had given permission, so it doesn't fall on my shoulders. Although this is my area and it probably should."

"Not if you had oversight permission. But who would know that the case would be open, Tasha?"

"The police asked the same question, and the list isn't very long," she said. "The councilman. His campaign director, Mark Renn. An assistant whose name I don't know. My director, Hume Morris, and the associate director, Gina Montgomery. She wasn't here that day. Hume was. And Jay, of course. We alert security whenever there's a change in display status, even if we're simply moving something from one place to another."

"So any one of those people could have told someone else."

She frowned. "Would they, though? About something sensitive, like an open display case?"

"You'd be amazed what people say in casual conversation. And even just having a tidbit overheard by another party can set things in motion. Most folks these days aren't as careful about what they say in public."

Tasha rolled her eyes. "Oh, there is a lot of truth in that, Julia. Too much."

"So it would be easy for someone to overhear a snatch of conversation that could lead to the theft."

"I guess." Worry darkened her gaze again. "It didn't seem like a lot of people at the time, but maybe that's because I really couldn't imagine someone stealing a bell collection. When things get stolen, it's usually for a purpose. But a forty-three-piece bell collection isn't easily fenced, right? Or moved. Not like a necklace or a ring." She shrugged. "Thank you for taking this on. I can't tell you how grateful I am. My brain feels like it's running in circles, and the spin is making me crazy."

"Because you're close to it," Julia said. "We have an outsider vantage point, and that's a different perspective. We need to go, but I would like to see the elevator too. The one that may have been used to take the bells downstairs."

"Of course."

Meredith fell into step beside Tasha while Julia concentrated on her watch. "Tasha, were they able to get any footage from the cameras on the street, along the lane or in the museum?"

"The inside ones were no help. The darkness factor messed that up, or the electrical outage. The street cameras were working, but there was nothing unusual, according to the police. The cameras that focus on the back of the building didn't work. A neighboring business camera did show a corner of a car that was parked in the lane at the right time but no identifying characteristics. Trees and garbage bins line the lane, and there are delivery trucks in and out of there all the time, but no good footage from anyone. They must have exited by going forward, and with that camera old and broken, there was nothing at all except the little shot of that gray car that could belong to anyone. The museum realizes they need to rectify that situation."

"Do a lot of delivery trucks use East Gordon Lane?" asked Julia as they approached the elevator. She reached forward and pushed the button for service.

"A few," replied Tasha. "The lane services a bunch of buildings."

"Is there a delivery log for that day?" wondered Meredith. "Because a driver could have witnessed something without realizing it was important."

"There's an on-site delivery log for the museum, but I don't know if the other buildings do that. And the small deliveries come through the side door, into the offices. They just pull up out front, block traffic, and dash in and out. We really don't get a lot of back-door deliveries here. Not like the other businesses. I can send you a copy of our delivery schedule. Wouldn't the police have checked this out?"

"Possibly, but if they're suspecting this was an inside job, the delivery vans and trucks probably aren't high on their investigative list." Julia looked up from her watch as the elevator slid to a somewhat noisy halt in front of them. "It took us thirteen seconds to get from the case to the elevator and thirty-two seconds for the elevator to come to this floor."

"That means this could have been done in forty-five seconds?" Tasha's brows shifted up. "That quickly?"

"Unless the perp had to carry the bells one box at a time," said Meredith. "Then we have to multiply the back-and-forth by three."

"And they're just stockpiling the bells here, waiting for the elevator?" Tasha sounded dubious, but Julia wasn't.

"It's all workable according to how long the lights were out up front, the confusion, the noise, the voices. You said folks were screaming at first?"

"Not for their lives, of course. But in shock. Alarmed. Calling out to one another and then turning on their cell phone flashlights, blinding each other. It was bedlam."

"For how many minutes?"

"At least two or three," she admitted. "We already had a problem because the protesters wouldn't leave when asked, and Jay was on the verge of calling the police when the lights went out."

"And where were you?"

"Near the councilman's event. I stood off to the side, keeping an eye on things and answering texts from Gina. Hume wasn't happy that she took the day off. It was clear he didn't think I was up to the job with Marion out on maternity leave, and the day's results seemed to prove him right."

The regular event coordinator out on leave, a scheduled event, a lot of people on hand when there had been a trickle prior to that because of the reconstruction in the east wing, the confusion of that reconstruction, and a scheduled protest. Julia hastened to reassure her. "This wasn't and isn't your fault, and if we work together, we'll figure this out, Tasha. The question is who was on-site that might have known about all these circumstances coming together?"

"I can't even imagine," answered Tasha. "It's a lot of information, and there's no one I can think of who would have been in on all the loops needed. And yet someone must have been. Or it was just dumb luck."

Meredith's lifted brow said she wasn't putting her money on luck of any sort.

"No one was anywhere near the elevator or this hallway?" Julia asked.

"Not that I know of. There wasn't a reason for anyone to be here. We weren't letting people into the rooms with the displays until after the councilman's address. It was scheduled that way deliberately."

"So all someone had to do was know that the bells were open and that no one would be down that hall." Julia glanced at Tasha for confirmation.

"Yes."

"That narrows the playing field substantially," Julia told her. "Because there are very few people from the councilman's staff who would know both things. That helps us zoom in."

"Oh good!" Relief softened Tasha's features. Her phone buzzed. She pulled it out of her pocket and raised it. "I have to take this. But thank you so much for coming by. Both of you. You have no idea how much this means to me, Julia. Just to know someone's on my side. It's everything." She hurried off.

Meredith led the way to the front door of the museum. "Ready for a little walk? I want to take a quick stroll and check out that lane firsthand."

"My thoughts exactly. Let's go. And if we get a little wet?" Julia eyed the thickening cloud cover. "We'll dry off back at the office."

Chapter Eighteen

"War or no war, I'll not go north to school." Bridie's fists were on her hips. "I understand what you're saying, but if our men go off to war, we'll need women to help run the farm and the mill." She didn't fold her arms or stomp her feet. She didn't often resort to childish expressions of strength, frankly because she didn't need to. Today was no exception. "I'm strong. I'm able. And I'm willing, Da."

She always reverted to the more Irish colloquial "Da" when she wanted to win approval she thought might not come. Lincoln's election had spurred South Carolina's declaration of secession and the subsequent Confederate attack on Fort Sumter. "You'll go north for safety's sake, if for no other reason," Brian told her. "I give you rein most often, Bridget Mary, but there will be no talk of you staying in Savannah now, with us not knowing what will come of all this."

"Horrible decimation, I expect," Bridie answered. "And all because of the lust for free labor."

"That's just the sort of talk that folks will jump on now, Daughter. The sort that could get you hurt. We've got like-minded folks around us." The majority of Savannah business owners weren't slave owners and had nothing to do with the slave trade, but the city's economy was affected by the health of some plantations, although not as much as when they first arrived.

"The boys will join up when they're of age and not as most Georgians would expect." She faced her father and spoke with a certainty that fourteen-year-olds rarely embraced. "I'll not be tucked away like some rare flower. If I must go north, send me to Cousin Derrick. I can work in the factory there. Outfit the troops or make bandages. I'm a good worker, Da. We know this."

She was, in fact. Hardworking, industrious, and uncannily bright, well-read before her time. Different from her brothers for good reason, but not one that would ever be spoken of. Here in America, she was their child. Their blood. And no one except a few family members thought otherwise.

Derrick Monaghan, the third of the smart ones, had emigrated a year after the rest of them. He'd chosen Yankee roots for his family and had started a garment manufacturing business in Philadelphia. "There's not a breath of fresh air to be had in that city, Bridget."

"There's a cause that will give me air enough, Da. Air to breathe freedom for others. Air to help free those around us. You said yourself that brokers are trying to wrench contracts here in the South and hand them off to weasels from overseas. Surely my uncle must be facing similar problems and can use all the help he can get to fill orders."

Brokers and lobbyists were doing that all over the country and the world, according to the short note Derrick's wife had sent. She didn't send it by telegraph, because prying eyes saw too much of those, and neither Derrick nor Brian wanted their businesses gutted. Brian had the wool.

Derrick and Jim had the garment manufacturing, one in the North, one in the South. If Brian was to step up production, he could help supply Derrick with high quality wool, necessary for military use. But should he try to get his wool to Derrick? England had sent yardage to the Richmond Depot, yardage in both blue and gray. So was it worth the risk to life and limb for his family?

"A dead producer helps no one, Husband."

Mary Kate's softly spoken words troubled him, for when did a man need to stand on principle?

"The gift of postwar jobs will be of better service than losing the mill," she added. Addressing Bridget, Mary Kate raised her voice. "Your father and I will send you to your uncle, and the work of your hands will be blessed with our prayers, just as it is for your brothers, although I expect schoolwork to be accomplished as well." The younger two boys would stay and work the mill, but the older boys were Unionists. They'd gone to Philadelphia and signed on with the Union army. That alone could have repercussions enough.

Bridie lifted her chin. Just enough to maintain respect but still show her independence. "When may I return?"

"When it is safe for our precious daughter to do so," said Brian firmly. "And if I could convince your mother to stay with you—"

"An impossible task," Bridie interrupted. She shared a firm look with her mother. "For she'll not leave your side, your cause, or our livelihood in less capable hands. And if lacemakers are left with no work, they'll busy their hands making uniforms for the military. Someone must keep the lace trade alive."

Thousands of women were busily sewing uniforms in all parts of the country. Independent laborers were taking piece-work on both sides of the great divide. While part of Derrick's business was run on machines, it took a person to work each machine and no small number of hand sewers. The fourteen-year-old's assertion was correct. Lace would take a necessary back seat while wool ruled the day, and Brian would need his wife's quite capable hands.

He accompanied both of his ladies to the train depot the next day. "This will take you to Wilmington," he reminded them as a porter loaded their bags and Bridie's trunk. From their exchanged looks, he knew he was repeating what he'd already said, but it was worth saying again. "Then on to Richmond—"

"Where we take the cross-route up to Alexandria, a packet to Washington, then up to Philadelphia. I'm Irish born, Husband." Mary Kate rolled her eyes at him. "I can find m'way onto a train car and off, thank ye kindly, and heaven knows if I lose my way, our daughter will no'."

His boys gone to war.

His wife accompanying his daughter to the relative safety of the North then returning because she was too stubborn and too skilled to turn her back on all they'd built.

His younger sons caught here, with him, where war might surely find them one day. He'd brought them here. To this. He'd done it deliberately, he and the cousins.

Your choice was starvation or freedom.

But freedom didn't come free. He'd known that in Ireland. He saw it here. The price of freedom would be dear, but not in his hands.

In God's. And in that he must trust. He saw his beloveds onto the train, made sure they had fruit, nuts, and bread in their bags, then watched the train roll north without him.

And then he went back to work.

Chapter Nineteen

THE WIND HAD PICKED UP and the feel of rain was in the air. A cold feel. When they turned toward East Gordon Lane, Julia paused and snapped a couple of quick pictures.

Garage-door delivery entrances lined both sides of the street once they got beyond the museum's gated wall. While James Oglethorpe, the founder of Savannah, had liked the use of the word *lane* to describe these access points, this one was more like an alley. Garbage bins lined one side, and there was no traffic nor were there deliveries being made currently. "Easy to see how someone could have pulled up here, had the bells put into a vehicle, and been gone quickly," Julia noted.

Meredith paused by the gate that broke up the brick wall protecting the museum grounds. She pointed toward the back door that opened for the elevator. "There's your access point leading to the elevator door." The museum's east and west courtyards offered an inviting green space on either side of the main building. "A one-minute walk to the car."

"Except the weight of the bells indicates a strong person, or two people, because those things aren't light." Julia studied the layout and frowned. "Even though they're packed in three cases, each case is hefty. And they're not in wheeled suitcases like modern bells would be. The pictures we have from the museum show old-fashioned leather-bound cases, made of wood. Nothing light about them."

"So then how did they manage it this quickly?" Meredith studied the layout. "Someone waiting at the door then running the cases to the vehicle, one by one?"

"That increases the time substantially, and the chance to be noticed, but maybe. It's plausible. That means we're talking three people coordinating this?"

"Three trips to the car would make it easier for the person to be noticed."

"Exactly," agreed Julia. "But here's the good thing. We've narrowed the list. I don't believe in the providence of luck in this case. There are too many factors. Let's go back to the office and come up with a Venn diagram and see what names fall in the middle. Then maybe we can set up a time with the choir director who actually used the bells. Maybe she's got an inkling of what's going on. She knew Rose Mulholland. There's a part of me that wonders how the bells' past is affecting their present. If at all."

"I'll call and see if I can schedule a time with her," said Meredith. "That way she's more likely to open the door. The last thing I want to do is frighten her, but she is the only one familiar with the bells other than the pastor, and he wasn't exactly in a hurry to talk to us."

They went straight back to the office, where fresh coffee awaited them, along with an overflowing gift basket from Miss Charlotte, the elderly and extremely wealthy head of the Delorme Foundation. She'd sought their help the year before with a case of mistaken identity.

Meredith's eyes widened when she spotted the basket.

Carmen swung around the corner of the kitchen, took a selfie with the gift, and then faced the women. "It weighs twenty-seven pounds."

"No." Meredith's eyes went even wider as she walked around the basket in astonishment.

"Oh yes." Carmen gave the immense gift a hug of affection. "It's not the wicker basket tipping the scales in that direction either. Chocolate, chocolate, and more chocolate."

"I am rarely gobsmacked," murmured Julia as she slipped off her jacket and hung it to dry over the kitchen heater. The rain had started as they walked back to their car, and while they didn't get soaked, they did get wet. "It's not only ginormous, it's all top names and specialty companies."

"Including a Lithuanian torte from a little shop in Omaha," said Carmen. "I can't see all the names, but that torte alone, with shipping, is nearly fifty bucks. ¡Aye caramba!"

"Did she send a card?" asked Meredith.

Carmen nodded. "Two, actually. One from Miss Charlotte herself and then a second one from Brenda James."

"That sweet assistant of hers is a treasure," noted Meredith. "She keeps things down to earth when Miss Charlotte gets a little too grand dame for the new millennium."

Carmen reached across the counter. She raised a festive card then read it aloud. "'To my dear new friends at Magnolia Investigations... I am thankful to know you and grateful for your help. Please accept this basket, the very same one I give to my best vendors and friends, as a token of my gratitude and respect. The contents reflect many of our fifty states' best treats from multiple ethnicities and kitchens, big and small. God bless you all and Merry Christmas!'" Then Carmen raised another notecard. "And this from Brenda. 'P.S.: Carmen, I loved chatting with you about your childhood and Guatemala! It brought back so many good memories of a time when I was young and carefree. I told the coffee shop on our block about Mexican Hot Chocolate and how delicious it is. They did a test run and agreed, and it's now on the drink menu. Hooray! Their new recipe is remarkably similar to what I had in Guatemala many years ago with just enough fire to make it interesting, so that gift card is for you. I hope it brings back good memories for you like it did for me.'"

"How sweet is that?" Julia smiled at Carmen. "Carmen, your work is affecting people in such a good way. Thank you."

Carmen waved off the compliment. "Maggie Lu is on her way. Have you two come up with a gift idea for her yet? Because I think I have. If you don't think it's too weird."

Julia and Meredith exchanged looks. They weren't generally the gag-gift type, but Julia wouldn't hurt Carmen's feelings for the world so she kept her tone easy. "Maggie Lu doesn't strike me as a 'weird gift' kind of person, Carmen."

Carmen rolled her eyes. "The *gift* isn't weird," she said. "It just might be weird for us to give it to her. Here." She handed them a computer printout from an online used clothing store. In the center of the page was a hat, the exact replica of the one Jacob had given his mother over twenty years before. "I know that hat meant a lot to her, and I know we can't really replace it, but when I saw this exact one, I thought it might be a nice—"

"Not *nice*," Meredith assured her with a smile and a half hug. "Way beyond nice. Perfect, Carmen."

"Can we get it here in time?" asked Julia.

Carmen nodded. "They say yes, but if the church can have twelve days of Christmas, I think we can too."

Julia laughed because Carmen was right. "Order it. And thank you so much for taking the time to do this. Can you order a bag of those Mary Jane candies too? I think she'd enjoy those."

"On it." Carmen folded the printout and tucked it beneath her arm. "You said you wanted to form a Venn diagram, so I set up the whiteboard in the conference room. Coffee's ready," she added as she moved back to her desk up front.

Julia headed toward the conference room. Meredith veered into her office first. By the time they all had coffee and slices of the melt-in-your-mouth Lithuanian torte, Maggie Lu had arrived.

She didn't walk in like she normally did.

She rushed in, hung her winter coat on the back of the chair, and took a seat. She clasped her hands and leaned forward. Excitement fairly oozed from her eyes. She didn't wait for a greeting, nor give one. She just dived right in with her news. "Those bells didn't come from the Peak family. Or the circus. They arrived shortly after the Mulhollands got here to set up shop in 1847. Shipped in on a vessel containing machinery for the original woolens factory. And with papers attached." She set a thin hardcover book down on the table with a slight *thunk*.

"1847?" Julia stared at her. "Shipped in?" It made no sense. None. Unless Mary Kate Mulholland really did love the bells and had them brought from Ireland? "If Mary Kate had them brought in, why were they stuck away so long? Unless maybe they weren't?" She frowned, thinking. "The numbers don't bear this out," she explained. She folded her hands. "Meredith is the history expert here, but Carmen's research showed an influx of Irish settlers into Savannah during the great famine, especially after the Northeast began blocking the Irish from entering or finding work. It wasn't long before they became one-third of Savannah's population. So if that's true, why weren't those bells used or donated to the early church that became St. Kieran's? Why would the Mulhollands go to the expense and trouble of shipping bells that no one would use?"

"Maggie Lu, how did you discover this?" Meredith lifted the book and read the title out loud. "*Living Free: A Collection of Essays and Articles* by Rudyard Simmons."

"It's the book I talked about before," Maggie Lu told them. "I couldn't bring the name to mind, it was so long ago that I read it, but I knew it mentioned Brian Mulholland and his wife, how they took care of people. I remembered how someone said they hired folks with no thought to skin tone. I found the book online and had a copy sent to the Bull Street branch. And I found this, page eighty-three." She indicated the bookmark in the slim volume. "What I found wasn't just the testimony of a good man for his employer. I found the bells."

Meredith put on her reading glasses, cleared her throat, and began to read.

Blue Collier, free man as told to this interviewer in 1889:
   "I was born a free man because my daddy and my mama were set free after the War of 1812. My daddy fought hard and my mama saved the lives of the mistress and her baby daughter, and so they were given papers. Emancipation papers. My daddy worked the docks, and then I worked the

docks with him until he passed. I worked with our own kind until Mr. Mulholland and his family come to town. I was thirty-one years old, and this man, this white man who was startin' a big company and hirin' workers, talked to me. Right to me, man to man. I wondered what would happen, you know, when he got told the rules, cuz he was new here. New to Savannah, and new to this country, but it never happened. He treated me like he would one of his own kind and offered me a job right off when I delivered a wagonload of machinery to his new mill.

"'Why don't you come work for me here?' he asked. 'I could use a smart, strong worker like you in the mill.' I said no at first because folks ain't like leopards. A leopard can't change its spots. Folks can. And what if I gave up my job at the docks and it didn't work out with this new fellow? So I said no, but he kept askin'. After the war, when his family had their youngest boy buried up North, I changed my mind and brought others with me to learn the trade of the woolens. He hired us on even when others got mad, saying that boys coming back from the war should get all the jobs. Mr. Brian would just look at them and say, 'These folks have been fighting a war all their lives, a battle to keep life and limb together. My men stay.'"

I interrupted Blue here because this wasn't the first praise testimony I'd heard about the Mulholland family. "He sounds like a good man," I said.

"Real good," Blue agreed, and then he continued his story. "Now Honey, my missus, she called him one of God's own, and I guess that's the most accurate. The mill kept us on until it was past retirement for all of us. A man's eyes say a lot *you know, and I read Mr. Brian's way back when I brought him that first load of goods up the hill to the mill."*

Blue took a moment here, lost in thought. I didn't hurry him. There was no need to. Then he brought a shaky hand to his chin. "I knowed what I knowed when we set things about, unloadin' those wagons. There was a different box, in a different hand, not labeled the same. Me and Mr. Jim Monaghan took it over to where Mr. Brian was standing with Miss Mary Kate. He used a bar to open it, and that crate was filled with boxes of bells. Fancy boxes, they were. And fancy bells, for ringing. Them bells were heavy, and so many of them it took three cases to hold them, all snug in their crates, bound with rope, as heavy and well packed as some of the machinery. He looked into that first box, and he was so surprised and determined it was a mistake and we should take them back. Figure out where they really belonged. We were about to do that when Mr. Jim found a leather pouch tucked down the side of the case. He handed it to Mr. Brian, and then Mr. Brian opened another case and found a note. Well, Mr. Brian read it to himself with the missus peekin' over his shoulder, and that man's whole face changed. He looked at his wife. She was standin' alongside, holding that pretty baby of theirs, and she looked at him, and he looked at her, and I swear he almost cried. Maybe both of them, even. She hugged that baby close, and her and Mr. Brian kind o' shared this look, like love and sadness all mixed up. I saw that and realized this might be a man I could trust one day. And I did. Later. When I dared."

"What happened with the bells?" I asked.

Blue shrugged. "Don't know hide nor hair. Never saw 'em again. Never heard them played, not when going by their church or anywhere, for that matter. I know he took 'em home, because he had us load 'em onto his wagon, and I saw him drive past me later that day, headin' to their place. But I knew from that day on that one day I'd work for Mr. Brian, and I never regretted one single minute of sayin' yes once the war was over. He made a difference, that one, and the rest of his family too. There wasn't a one of them I wouldn't trust with my life, and when young Bridie got her fancy education and set up a doctorin' business up North and helped get rights for folks and the vote for women, I cheered her on like she was one of my own because that's how it was with the Mulhollands. They made you feel like one of their own."

"Oh my." Julia grabbed a tissue and dabbed her eyes carefully so she wouldn't mess up her mascara. "Maggie Lu, what a beautiful interview. It's like turning a page and seeing history come to life."

"And he saw the bells when Brian Mulholland opened them," Maggie Lu declared. "That doesn't jibe with anything ever said about them in all this time."

"Shipped directly from Ireland," added Carmen.

"But then how did that story about Barnum and the Peaks and all that other ever get started?" wondered Meredith. "That's what's always been shared. But then that wouldn't be the first rumor that's taken on wings of its own," she added as she studied the book more carefully.

"So what was in that note that got them all emotional, I wonder," mused Julia. As she spoke a chill grabbed hold of her. An icy chill that seemed to come from inside.

"Were the bells a gift?" suggested Meredith.

"Maybe played at their wedding in Ireland?" offered Maggie Lu. "Or a family heirloom?"

Julia tugged her sweater more snugly around herself as she acknowledged Maggie Lu's idea. "It could be that simple. Something that brought old memories, a beloved country, missing their former life."

Meredith seemed skeptical. "Except that even though Brian Mulholland loved his homeland, he constantly spoke against the use of indentured servants to keep rich English landlords in furs and regal homes while the Irish countryside perished. There are multiple historical interviews with Brian and Mary Kate and other members of the Mulholland and Moynihan clans. The major theme the interviews have in common is the family's sympathy for the downtrodden. In fact," Meredith continued, "Mary Kate not only trained women of all colors how to make lace, just like she did in Ireland, she also sponsored the first Catholic school in the area. She made sure blue-collar people got a chance to go to the school because she felt their education wasn't strong enough. It took a while before a solid elementary education became the norm in Georgia. That school's results helped elevate schools across Savannah and the state because those sisters set the bar high."

A giving family. A big family. "So the stories of them being wonderful, industrious, and fair people are accurate." Julia tapped a fingernail on the tabletop. "But the stories surrounding the bells are not. Why? Why would someone invent a story about something that apparently almost moved them to tears?"

"Crime?" Carmen posed the question simply. "Maybe they'd done something illegal in Ireland and they came here for a fresh start. Maybe the bells weren't a reminder of good times but of bad choices?"

"You might be onto something," said Meredith. "I hadn't thought of it, but that would be a good reason to put the bells away and offer a totally different explanation for them. I can use the historical databases at the library to do a deep search. I did it for the historical society often enough, and maybe we can find out if there's a shadow in the Mulhollands' past. I'll get right on that tomorrow."

"And that could be why the bells have gone missing now," added Julia. "If there's a scandal attached to them, maybe someone feared it would get out."

"And who's got the most to lose in the Mulholland family if scandal gets out?" asked Meredith, but you could tell she didn't like posing the question.

Julia hated to say it, but it was the elephant in the room. "Councilman Hank Mulholland Webster."

Chapter Twenty

CARMEN FOLDED HER ARMS AND frowned. "Why on earth would something that happened a hundred and seventy years ago be a problem now?" She looked around the table. "It's not that I don't think the past matters. It does. But if there's some almost two-hundred-year-old heinous crime in Mulholland history that can wipe out all the good they did, I say leave it be. Haven't they paid their dues?"

"I can't disagree with that," Maggie Lu said. "But we won't know until Meredith does her digging. And until then, I need to get on." She stood and reached for her rain slicker. "I'm meeting Rebecca for a little shopping time, and then we're having supper at the diner. With so many folks taking holiday dinner cruises, that sweet-talking hubby of hers is working every night and twice on weekends. He says he'll spend the winter resting his voice to jump back on board in March."

Rebecca Thompson worked at the Carnegie branch of the library, and her husband Kelvin was one of the historical emcees on the dinner cruises. Kelvin was often referred to as the Voice of Savannah—a title he loved. According to Kelvin, preserving his voice was the reason he never yelled at sporting events, not because he didn't care but because one must always take care of one's assets.

Julia stood too because they needed to get their Venn diagram done, but the moment she did, her legs went to rubber.

She paused, hands on the desk, and took a breath.

The breath felt tight. Real tight. Like it didn't quite make its way to her lungs because she didn't have the strength to push it past the thickness in her throat.

Carmen had crossed to the whiteboard. She raised a dry erase marker and turned, but the moment she saw Julia, she hurried around the table. "What is it? What's wrong?"

Julia shook her head. "Don't know," she finally whispered, but it didn't sound like her whispering. The voice sounded far away. And weak. And Julia's voice was never weak. "Feel bad. Really bad, all of a sudden." That was all she could say.

Another chill raced along her spine. Then another. At the same time her face broke out in a sweat.

"I'm calling Beau." Meredith reached for her phone.

Julia couldn't argue. Didn't dare argue. She pointed to her throat.

Carmen helped her back into her seat while Maggie Lu hurried to the first aid cupboard in the bathroom. She brought back a small pharmacy of over-the-counter meds. "Julia, does your throat feel tight?"

Julia nodded. That was all she could do. What she wanted was a pillow and seventeen blankets as the chills raced from her toes right up to the top of her head.

"An allergic reaction?" wondered Meredith as she called Beau. She looked worried. Maggie Lu and Carmen looked worried too, which meant Julia was scaring them, but she couldn't find words to tell them she'd be all right. Besides, right now she wasn't sure that was the truth.

"Girl, you are burning up," declared Maggie Lu as she put a hand to Julia's forehead.

Carmen rushed down the hall and came back with her jacket and car keys. "I'll take her home. The morning news said the flu is a rough one this year and comes on like you got hit by a ton of bricks."

Julia didn't try to argue with the accurate assessment. Her head hurt, her chest was tight, and her throat felt rough and hot. "I haven't had the flu in ten years." She let Carmen help her into her coat. "It appears my run of good immunity is over. Keep me posted?"

Meredith stayed a wise distance away and waved her on. "Will do. Your only job right now is to get well. I'll let Beau know you're coming and we can get your car to you later."

Julia heard her, but the words didn't mean a great deal.

How did she go from feeling quite well one minute to feeling like a freight train had just broadsided her?

She got home.

Beau took her right into the Quick Care, where they diagnosed the flu, prescribed medications and bed rest, and sent her home. That was exactly where she stayed for six long days. By the time she was well enough to get back to work the following Tuesday, she'd missed four holiday get-togethers that she didn't regret, Kennedy's play that she did regret, and was glad she'd done her holiday shopping early. Christmas was a few days away, and the last thing she wanted was for Tasha to be worried about going to jail. Meredith had uncovered two things in Julia's absence. First, she discovered that Tasha hadn't answered her phone for nearly six minutes during the theft, a crucial time when Hume was trying to contact her.

And Tony Carlisle had worked for Kevin Mulholland, Hank's cousin, two years before, a history he hadn't bothered to mention while discussing his disappearing act the week before.

She came into work the following week, slung her bolero-style jacket onto the hook, and headed for her office, determined. She'd lost days of investigation time. Meredith's deep search through the library archives turned up nothing—neither branch of the family, the Mulhollands nor the Monaghan/Moynihans, had a breath of scandal to their names.

So why those bells?

Why now? What kind of significance did they hold? And for whom?

If Hank masterminded this disappearance, what was the purpose? It wasn't money. That initial thought had been taken care of and explained away.

Fiona had nothing to gain by taking the bells, except some sort of decades-old vengeance against her grandmother for giving them away, but that made little sense.

Tasha needed money. Badly. That gave her motive and opportunity, and the police had uncovered that six-minute stretch of time where she didn't answer her phone when the boss was calling her.

Then again, with the lights going out and the chaos of everyone screaming and running around like chickens with their heads cut off, who could blame her?

Julia set up coffee to brew. Meredith and Carmen had somehow escaped catching the flu from her, thank heavens, but Maggie Lu was down with it now. Beau was leaving cups of layered Jell-O and chicken soup on her porch, two of the few things Julia ate after the initial awful seventy-two hours.

Meredith and Carmen joined her a half hour later. "Julia!" Carmen squealed but kept her distance. "I'm not hugging you just in case you're still sick, but I'm so glad you're here. You looked so bad last week!"

"Sure did," said Meredith. She crossed over and fist-bumped Julia. "I got your text about going full steam ahead."

"I'm totally set on making up for lost time," Julia replied.

"Well, the problem with that is that the rest of the world generally grinds to a halt Christmas week and tends to stay that way until January second," Meredith reminded her. "We'll do what we can, but it's a tough go out there. Other than retail, a lot of places take vacation or go with shortened hours, and the flu spread has made it worse."

Julia pointed to the blank whiteboard. "No luck with the Venn diagram?"

"It just wasn't helpful," Meredith said. "I keep thinking there's one person we haven't been able to talk to." She looked at Julia with raised brows.

Julia met her gaze. "The one person we haven't been able to talk to who might actually know something about the bells is Tallie O'Meara, the choir director. She knew Rose, and she knew the bells. Let's get our foot in the door of her house. She might be the only living person who knows anything about them, so let's see if she can shed some light on why someone would want them. And in the meantime, Carmen, can you find out everything you can about the donation of the bells from the church to the museum?"

"Glad to. I'll get right on it."

Meredith glanced at the clock. "Most elderly people I know like to get up early and catch a quick rest later. We probably shouldn't surprise her. Knowing how well that worked last time." She made a face that underscored how poorly they'd fared trying to pop in on the aged woman.

"I'll call," said Julia. "It's time to ring her bell."

Carmen groaned. "That was really, really bad."

Julia laughed. "It was. But let's see if it works."

Chapter Twenty-One

Savannah, Georgia
Christmas, 1865

War over.

    City spared.

    Farm intact.

    Work continues.

    Blessed Christmas, my love.

Brian sent the telegram to Mary Kate on the twenty-third of December. She'd gone north to spend Christmas with their precious daughter while he stayed home to keep the mill running.

There was much he couldn't say.

They'd lost one son to the war and one to the North. Liam would stay in Pennsylvania, charting a new path with a Northern wife whose father grew sheep. The loss of his second-born son would be keen at the mill.

Joe would return. As would Mary Kate and Bridget.

Alec had stayed in Savannah to help run the factory, and there'd been no small number of jeers from certain quarters. But wool was essential, and while many jobs were well handled by women, the pulling apart of gears and machinery sometimes required a man's strength.

But Michael...

Michael, the youngest of his sons, a kind boy who saw keenly and felt deeply, had been lost in one of the final battles of Petersburg. Gunned down just months after he'd gone to service.

Gone to one of the tens of thousands of graves littering a new nation.

Brian couldn't bear to think of it. Of how close they'd come to losing no one. A matter of months separated his beloved son from the line of heaven and earth.

His heart ached, and when his heart ached, the only thing he knew was work. Work helped. It didn't sustain. God did that, the blood of the Lamb.

But work helped, and with that thought he and Alec kept working under the oddest of conditions. Union soldiers everywhere. Cries of victory. Cries of defeat. But as he and a crew worked to clean and create the first fabrics of the about-to-be-reunited union, a whistle came.

He went to the window.

Blue stood in the roadway alongside the mill. Brian shoved open the window. A sharp blast of cold air filled the room. Cold enough to feel different. Sharp enough to almost feel good. "Hello, Blue."

"I've come about the offer," the man called up from below. He motioned to two men standing back a ways. Dark-skinned men, both wearing the hollowed look of hunger. "I've come to work, Mr. Brian."

He should turn them away.

He should advise the hardworking docker to come again once things settled down. But there was no indication of that happening anytime soon. None.

So how could they know when things would settle? And wasn't this exactly what his son had given his life for? So that men of all colors could be free to earn a living? "I'm in need," he called back. "Meet me below." And then, so his meaning would be abundantly clear, he motioned behind Blue. "All three of you."

Mary Kate would be proud of him. As would Bridie. As long as he didn't get killed for his action. But with the army milling about, that was unlikely. And by the grace of God, the hand up to good workers was what would rebuild the South eventually. Yes, Sherman had spared the city the demolition of torches, but the blockades had ruined trade and their economy for four long years.

Not his, so much. That was a different kind of guilt. The need for woolens had only intensified with time, and he'd increased the size of the mill and would soon upgrade his machinery, once equipment became available.

He was wealthier than when the first shots were fired, and he'd lost a beloved child.

He hated war, but he loved freedom more than he hated war, and so they would go on. Without his curly-locked son whose quick wit and bright smile charmed a room.

He'd be charming heaven's quarters now, and there they would meet again. Someday.

Chapter Twenty-Two

Forty minutes later Tallie O'Meara opened her front door as Meredith and Julia walked down the sidewalk, and the first word that came to Julia's mind was *adorable*.

She was a smallish woman with bright blue eyes and unusually curly hair for an older person. The curls fit her pixie-like face and the quick smile. If the Hallmark Channel wanted a quintessential cute grandma in a movie, Tallie O'Meara fit the bill.

Julia had called and left a message, telling the elderly choir director that they were trying to help Hank Mulholland and thought maybe she could shed some light on the matter for them.

Tallie nudged the screen open while simultaneously keeping a curious cat from sneaking through the door with her foot.

"Ms. O'Meara." Julia smiled at her once they got in the door. "Thank you for meeting with us. We're grateful for your time."

"Not a soul in this world calls me anything but Tallie, except for a few who call me Mrs. M, which makes no sense since my last name begins with *O*, but you know how kids are. They get something in their heads and they run with it."

"They sure do," agreed Meredith.

Another cat appeared, an amber-eyed short-haired tabby. Tallie tucked them both onto a screened back porch. "Go chase sunbeams," she ordered them, but it was clear the cats were beloved friends, because the porch was a feline haven.

Cat cushions.

Cat pillows.

Twin scratching posts that looked brand-new and two old chairs that appeared well scratched.

A stand-up log for scratching or climbing.

A self-watering water dish.

And three cat-themed carpets covered parts of the tile.

Tallie slid the connecting door shut then came back their way. "They love their room. I decided long ago that I was not going to leave all my earthly goods to a cat or cats," she declared. "But I do intend to encourage the two I have to live their best lives here. So, ladies, what can I do for you? In your message you said there's a problem with Rosie's grandson, Hank?"

"Well, there's a number of problems and not just with Hank, actually," declared Meredith in her warm Southern tone. "Others too, what with the Mulholland bells going missing from the museum earlier this month, but Hank's the one that's got us most concerned. Being a city representative and all, we just want to make things right for him. Such a good, good man."

Julia let Meredith take the lead because she was good at playing the Southern belle. Julia didn't count schmoozing as one of her personal skills.

"Then there's Fiona, worried about this, that, and the other thing."

Julia watched Tallie's reaction to Meredith's words, and it was clear that Tallie wasn't wooed by sympathy for Fiona.

"And Reverend Martin over at your former church seemed surprised by the bells' disappearance from the museum."

Tallie looked doubtful. She folded her arms. "He seemed glad to be rid of them and the choir once, so I don't think he's sitting over there losing sleep about those bells now. It was an awful thing he did, giving them away like that when Rose intended them for the church, but you never know what a new pastor might do.... He didn't say a word to anyone about the decision, he just made it. And when I asked him about it, do you know what he said?" She didn't pretend to be a fan of the man. "'The church might like democracy, Mrs. O'Meara, but the church is *not* a democracy. There is much to be learned and loved at a quiet service, and the unfortunate truth is that my ears could not abide those bells.'"

"Quiet as in—no music?" asked Meredith.

Tallie nodded. "Music hurts his ears. Or so he said. He said he's been like that all his life and no amount of striving to overcome it has helped." She sighed. "In any case, change happens. We adjust. I was blessed to find a lovely church not far from here, so that worked out. No bells," she said, and shrugged. "But heart-stirring music. I sang with the choir until I got too old to carry the notes. Now I sing in the pew."

"Music speaks to my heart and soul," said Julia.

Tallie smiled. "Mine too."

"So, Tallie." Meredith hunched forward, and her expression invited confidentiality. "What is it about those bells that would make someone want to steal them? What are we missing? I can't find any historical significance connected with them to make them a collector's item. I don't see any scandal attached, and I feel like I've hit a brick wall. They're worth something only if they can be sold, but the bell market is quite small. We thought if there was something we were missing, you'd be the best person to talk with because you knew Rose and the bells. You knew them best. If there's anything you can tell us, we'd be so glad to hear it."

Tallie didn't answer right off. She motioned to the adjacent kitchen. "I have cookies and tea. My sugar cookies were voted the Number One Very Best at the Northern Savannah Cookie Exchange five years back, and it's a designation I take great pride in. Come on in the kitchen. It's always easier to talk in a kitchen, isn't it?"

Julia couldn't disagree. "I'm always most at home in the kitchen. A body doesn't have to wonder what to do with their hands when there's a table sitting right there." The ladies stood and followed her.

The kitchen was retro chic. Tallie had an eye for tucking things around a room that embraced the homey look, and as Meredith came into the kitchen, she squealed over a collection of kitchen-themed wall hangings. "Oh, I love this! I know the current trend is toward minimize, minimize, minimize, but I just love a home that isn't afraid to have things on the walls or shelves. How sweet is this? But land sakes, Tallie, how do you keep it all dusted? Especially up above there." Meredith pointed up while Julia swept the room a more studied look.

It wasn't cluttered, but it was busy. Far too busy for Julia's taste, but a collection of photographs on a bookshelf unit and the adjacent wall made her smile. A wealth of graduation pictures filled that area, with extra shots on several taken with various family and friends.

"That's my 'testimony to education' corner," Tallie told them as she set out a tin of thickly frosted cookies. Festive sprinkles brightened the white frosting on some while others had red, green, and gold sparkling sugar crystals. She'd likely used the coarser kind that cost a pretty penny but were a wonderful addition on frosted cookies. Julia's mom had bought them and used them lavishly with Wyatt's girls every time they made sugar cookies together. "My six granddaughters, high school and college. Well, three of them from college, the others are still attending, but they'll all be graduates in eighteen months, and that's the first generation of O'Mearas to all attend university. I taught fourth grade," she explained. She'd crossed to a chair and gripped the back. "I taught for thirty-six years then subbed for four more until I realized it was time to retire for real. I still had my church and my choir and the bells. Practices three days a week to cover all the services, and what a blessing it was, directing good, fine people."

"Like being home," suggested Meredith in a tone of compassion and empathy.

"Just like that," Tallie said as she sank into the chair opposite Julia. "It was my home away from home, but then change happens whether we like it or not, and I moved on. Although my family says I got hounded out."

"Did you? I'd be sorry to hear that's the case." Julia accepted a cookie when Tallie tipped the tin her way.

"Yes, but I was old enough and maybe wise enough to realize that if the changes there didn't suit me, the sweet Lord put a lot of opportunities in my path. And I'd inherited my parents' place out here by then, and maybe I was ready to be done with a twenty-minute drive into the city, especially at night. My eyes aren't what they were."

"So you were raised out here?" asked Julia.

"Yes. I moved to the city when Donald—my late husband—and I both got teaching jobs back before they paid well. We raised our three kids in a house not far from St. Kieran's, and while others folks admired the big, beautiful cathedral, Donnie and I liked the small-town feel of being near the water. A walking area, that neighborhood. It was very different from living out here," she added with a wave of her hand. "But fifty-five years has changed that too, and I'm within walking distance of six new neighborhoods that have popped up as farmland sold off. Most all these neighborhoods sprouted up while I was in the city, so it's different here too. But nice."

"You've seen a lot of change," noted Meredith.

Tallie nipped off a tiny corner of her cookie in a very ladylike fashion. "Mostly good for someone with an open mind to development. I think that's why Rose and I got a kick out of watching Hank grow up. She used to say he's got the soul of a lion and the heart of his great-great-grandmother Bridie. He surely did get her gift for words, and that's why he's doing so well in politics, you know. Rose always said it was meant to be. She thought it was God's wish, and she encouraged that boy every step of the way until she was gone."

"He was a favorite." Would being her favorite be enough to push Hank to get back the bells?

"Rose Mulholland didn't play favorites," Tallie said firmly. "It would have gone against her teachings and her whole self. She liked fair play, so she treated them the same, from scoldings to praisings, but I have to say that Fiona got more scoldings because, land sakes, that girl liked to argue everything from every which direction. She never could see, or didn't want to see, an opposing point of view, and that made trouble between the cousins, because Fee liked to start fights."

Not much had changed that Julia could see. "An instigator."

"She was that. I used to pray for her to soften her ways. Soften her heart. At least try to be kind and good. She talks a good game. That's what Rose used to say about Fee," she added. "But she's got no staying power, and for a woman to make it in this world, she needs staying power. For Fee, everything was someone else's fault, always. And I expect it still is, though I haven't seen her in a long, long time."

"Was there anything amazing about the bells, Tallie?" Meredith posed the question with care. "Something that would make them stand out or target them to be stolen?"

"Nothing," Tallie said, and she sounded regretful. "Oh, they're beautiful, all right, and their sound is incomparable. A bell choir that's skilled in the ringing and pausing of the bell's tremor creates a music that has no compare. Their value is in being wonderfully handcrafted, probably in Scotland or England, but what upsets me is all the rumors that people make up about them."

"We have heard a few things we've wondered about," said Meredith.

"According to Rose, those bells didn't come from a circus or a troupe or any other such thing that was occasionally said. I was particularly miffed when the museum put that on the bell exhibit, because it flat-out wasn't true, but they didn't want to hear from me, so I left it."

"What else did Rose tell you about the bells?" asked Julia as she reached for another cookie.

"She said that the bells had sat untouched for over a century in the attic of the Harris Street house, and that regardless of what kind of family significance they may have had, it was time they were played. And that's when she donated them to the church and we expanded the first choir to be a bell choir as well. Oh, it was a time of music and beauty in that church, I tell you." The smile that graced the old woman's face made Julia's heart open. Then the smile faded. "But things change. And we change with them. I'm sorry I can't help you any more," she added, and she sounded truly regretful. "I'd do anything to hear those bells played again. Fortunately my memory is what it is and I can revisit those sweet services in my head, anytime. The blessing of old age without memory issues." Her smile dimmed slightly. Then returned. "Is there anything else I can help you with?"

"The recipe for this frosting, for starters," gushed Meredith. "I've never had better, and it's surely not the plain water and sugar combination so many use."

"I'll write it right down for you," said Tallie, and she did. She handed it to Meredith a few minutes later.

The ladies stood. "Thank you for seeing us, Tallie," Julia said.

"It's a pleasure to meet two such fine ladies, doing detective work like you are."

When they got back on the road, Meredith chuckled. "Detectives, eh?"

Julia grinned. "I might have used that word in my message. I did say we were looking into things about the bells and wanted to help Hank. I didn't mention the agency, but I was hoping maybe she watches BritBox or Acorn and that would get her attention."

"I saw a chemo hat on a shelf in the kitchen," said Meredith.

Julia drew a quick breath. "You did?"

Meredith nodded. "I thought her curls were so cute, but when I saw the hat, I realized the curls were a wig. They're so well-made now that you can't even tell they're not real."

"That explains her expression when she mentioned not having memory problems."

"Her problems lean to physical, for certain. Well, God love her for seeing us. Fighting cancer isn't easy. You and I have seen enough of that in our years to know it's a rugged battle. And yet she was spry and good-spirited, so maybe she's handling the chemo just fine. Other than the hair loss."

Carmen's dance-friendly ringtone sounded. Julia answered the call on the Bluetooth connection. "Hey, Carmen. What's up?"

"The reverend is what's up, ladies. The reverend who donated the bells to the museum, to be precise."

"Reverend Martin that took over at St. Kieran's?"

"Reverend Martin who was paid the pretty sum of twenty-two thousand four hundred dollars for the Mulholland bells."

"He was what?" Meredith's mouth dropped open. "He told everyone he donated them. Are you sure?"

"The woman at the museum sent me a photo of the bill of sale," Carmen said. "The theft has revealed some kind of cover-up at the museum."

"Twenty-two-thousand dollars. Plus," breathed Julia.

"But wouldn't the money from the sale show up in the church's coffers that year? Wouldn't that be kind of obvious?" mused Meredith.

"Only if the money went into the church's accounts," replied Carmen.

Could the gruff man have pocketed the money? Hidden it away?

"He could have covered up about the origins of the money," suggested Julia. "Unless someone saw the actual check, they'd believe whatever was written down in the church ledger, wouldn't they? So it could have been designated as a memorial gift. A will bequest."

"Or he has a private stash somewhere to buffer his retirement." Carmen's frank assessment could have merit because money didn't just appear and/or disappear from church funds.

"I still can't get over the fact that he lied. Straight out. To his people." Meredith frowned as she took a right turn onto the two-lane.

"Which means we go pay Reverend Martin a quick visit. See what he has to say about it."

"I'm only sorry the quickest way back isn't the expressway," Meredith muttered when Carmen had disconnected the call. "Speed might take the snark off what I want to say."

"Or we go with your wealth of Southern charm. You're much better than I am at spreadin' sugar. So let's go see if we can find out what the good reverend has been up to. Once and for all."

Chapter Twenty-Three

"At some point, I want a chance to be the snarky one." Meredith slowed the car as the light began to turn and sent Julia a quick look. "But I'm glad to have the truth come out about those bells. After meeting Tallie O'Meara, the thought of this guy selling them off and pocketing the returns is abhorrent, but the fact that he did that doesn't bring us any closer to finding the bells. He already made his money. He might be a jerk, but he wasn't in the market to steal the bells back."

"True."

Meredith tapped the steering wheel as they waited for the light to change. "It is annoying that we've discovered pretty much nothing. Who stands to gain the most by having the bells?"

"No one unless they fence them. And that brings us back to the theft being an inside job. Only Tasha and other museum coordinators would know where to market something like that. It's not exactly general information, you know? And yet I don't believe any of them would do it."

The light turned green, and Meredith drove on. "I just can't figure out what we're missing."

Julia sighed. "I'm in desperate need of a caramel macchiato. I took off four pounds being sick, so I'm spending the holidays not worrying about calories and not going to any parties or gatherings that don't involve family. Doctor's orders," she added, smiling. "So coffee now. Then we pop in on the reverend. Then let's put our heads together and see what we're missing. It's almost Christmas, and you know I don't want to work Christmas Eve."

"Me neither. Let's grab coffee at the Bean and go on from there. If you order online, we can save time."

"I'm on it." Ten minutes later Julia dashed into the coffee shop then dashed back out. The rain that had begun as a chilly mist was now a drizzle, gray and gloomy.

"Jules, I'm so sorry you got wet," Meredith exclaimed when Julia slid back into the car, balancing the drink tray in one hand. "I don't want you to get sick again."

"I'm pretty sure rain doesn't cause illness, but I do appreciate the concern." She smiled at Meredith as she handed her coffee over. "It's so nice to feel better, but I can't tell you how much I hated losing time on all of this. It's tough enough being up against a hard break like Christmas, but once I was healthy enough to think again, all I could see was Tasha and those boys, dealing with this hanging over her head. My one goal was to make sure she had this off her shoulders by Christmas, and that isn't likely to happen now, so that's a disappointment. But we'll forge on and get it solved one way or another. Eventually."

Meredith tucked her to-go cup into the holder then eased back out into traffic. She made the turn toward the waterfront before she addressed Julia's comments. "It's so easy for us to feel like everything is on our shoulders, isn't it?" she asked gently. "I told you earlier about how I used to take on every assignment, how I said yes to everyone who needed my help."

Julia couldn't disagree. She was guilty of similar choices. "I hear you. Why am I having such a difficult time saying no these days?"

"When you were an overworked judge, you could say no to people and figure they understood. Nowadays you're afraid they'll think badly of you if you say no, aren't you?" She took her eyes off the road just long enough to raise her brows at Julia. "Especially in December."

Her words hit home. "You nailed it. I used to get away with not helping with things because I was working. And I worked a lot. So did Beau. Everyone accepted it. But now, being retired, I got guilted into saying yes to everything. And then taking over in my typical run-the-world fashion. But I'm missing the important things."

"Like just being still. Taking time. Thanking God." Meredith took one last turn toward St. Kieran's. "We Martha-types tend to put that on the back burner. I think that's why Maggie Lu is so good for us. She reminds us that even though there's work to be done, there are prayers to be prayed. And I need that reminder. Especially at Christmas."

"So I'm not crazy?" asked Julia.

Meredith laughed as she pulled into the church parking lot. It was empty save for one blue sedan. "I didn't say that. But no crazier than I am, which is why we've been buds for so long. We go through things together."

Julia took a small sip of her macchiato. It was still too hot to enjoy, but that one sip held promise. "Let's go find the pastor. Umbrellas up!"

A sign on the office door listed hours that indicated the church should be staffed now, but no one came to the door when Julia knocked.

"Let's try the rectory and the school," she said. The adjacent school had offered a fine education for many youngsters. It had closed years before and hadn't been reopened or rented. It was locked up tight, so they moved to the former rectory. This building had been modernized and separated into office units for several not-for-profit agencies. Two of the offices were closed. One had a sizable FOR LEASE sign on the front window, and the other office had a SAVE THE TREES CONSERVANCY sign. That office held a real live person. Julia tapped lightly on the door. The woman looked up and motioned them in.

They parked their umbrellas in the hall and stepped inside.

"We hate to bother you because we're not here to help save trees, although we both love trees," Julia assured the woman. "Just so we don't misrepresent ourselves."

The woman laughed. "Point taken. What can I help you with?"

"We're looking for the pastor of the church next door."

"You and a lot of other people," replied the woman. "I can't tell you how often I have folks wandering in here, needing to connect with the church or the pastor. There's rarely anyone there except for Mr. Hopkins, and he isn't around all that much lately, either. It's even sparse on Sunday mornings when I drive by. I'm sorry I'm not more help. I do know he drives a gray sedan, and he usually parks on the far side of the church on the road. That way if folks don't see his car in the parking lot, they drive on by."

"Seriously?" Meredith's brows shot up.

"I am quite serious," the woman said. "One of the members stopped by a week or so ago and told me that. He also said the minister is retiring as of the first of the year. They're not sure if there'll be a replacement with numbers so low. He seemed sad, and I was sorry to see it. I do have the pastor's number, though." She jotted down a phone number and handed it to Julia. "We all exchanged numbers in case of an emergency. Well, he didn't give us his number, but the secretary did. She did mention that it was above her pay grade to have to run interference for him 24/7."

"A phone tree," said Meredith.

"Exactly. There's only a dozen of us on it, but it's efficient."

Efficient and useful. Julia raised the slip of paper as she headed for the door. "You've been a big help. At least this way we can text him if we can't locate him. Thank you so much, and Merry Christmas!"

"The same to you ladies. And if you could get the word out that choir practice isn't here, that would be helpful. I've had two young folks stop by this week, wondering where it was being held, which is curious, because I didn't think the old place has a choir. Not since I've been here, anyway."

"The office hours are messed up too," noted Meredith. "Sounds like he needs someone to keep things straight for him."

"Could be."

They grabbed their umbrellas and went back outside. The rain hadn't increased, but it hadn't lessened either. "Car, or a quick wet stroll around the church to see if he's here?" asked Julia.

"We've got umbrellas and comfy shoes. A little winter walk will do us good," replied Meredith. "And I want to know why there's a sudden interest in a choir for a church that has no choir, Julia."

"I had that very same thought," Julia replied. "Do you think they're practicing for a different church? But then why would they come here, looking for a practice that doesn't exist?"

"It's weird, isn't it?"

"Extremely." They circled the church until they came back to their parking space. No gray sedan was parked anywhere.

"So we text him," said Julia. She closed her umbrella, put it on the floor of the back seat and withdrew her phone. NEED TO SEE YOU ABOUT TRANSFER OF BELLS TO MUSEUM. LOOKING FORWARD TO YOUR QUICK RESPONSE. MAGNOLIA INVESTIGATIONS.

"Do we know where he lives?" wondered Meredith.

"No, and there's no listing on the web for him, which means he carries a really low profile. I would have asked if anyone had been in the office, but—"

"There was no one in the office."

"We've got his number. Maybe knowing we're looking into the transfer of the bells will jump-start something."

"Except there's no reason for him to steal the bells, so it's really no help to us if it does," noted Meredith. "But maybe it can bring some injustice to light."

Meredith parked behind the agency. They took their umbrellas inside to dry and left them on the steps leading down to the basement.

Carmen was up front. She heard them come in and met them in the hall. "I put together a timeline of the day the bells went missing." She preceded them into the conference room. "And I slapped together PB&J sandwiches for sustenance. The slide show of museum images from the alley security cameras is up, and you can magnify them. I wasn't able to get much more on that gray car behind the museum."

Gray car?

Meredith and Julia exchanged looks. "The unhappy pastor drives a gray car."

"So do a lot of people," said Carmen, "so that doesn't exactly pinpoint him."

"Not from a numbers perspective," said Julia. "However, if we want to erase suspicion from Tasha and put it on the guy who made money off the sale of donated bells, it works for me." She spoke in jest but with a hint of meaning.

Carmen laughed affectionately. "You always were known for rooting for the underdog, Julia."

"You're right," Meredith announced from her seat at the table. She was examining something on her laptop's screen. "There's no way to tell anything from this image except that it's a gray sedan."

"Nondescript gray car: check." Julia slipped into the chair at the end of the table. She set the remains of her coffee down and opened her laptop just as Rebecca Thompson came through the front door.

"I've brought cookies to go with your lunch," Rebecca announced as she came down the hall. "Carmen informed me that it's been a whole day since anybody's brought any goodies, and I don't want you wasting away." She paused at the door to the conference room and noted her wet shoes with a glance. "I'm not coming in there with wet shoes, so someone come and get this from me." She held out a cookie tin. "And," she added as Julia crossed the room, "when I talked to Maggie Lu earlier, she said she's feeling better and hopes to enjoy something more than broth and gelatin by Christmas. But if she's not, she'll have a Christmas dinner with Charlene and her crew on New Year's. She's been missing that great-grandbaby. Here you go." She handed Julia the Dickens-themed round tin. "I got this recipe from my old friend Tallie O'Meara years ago, and she makes the best cookies."

Meredith and Julia exchanged looks. "You know Tallie?" asked Meredith.

"I sure do," Rebecca replied. "We go way back to when I had little kids and she was the sage, older mom on the block who taught us not to sweat the small stuff. What a gift of common sense she was and still is. She's one of those folks you wish would live forever, you know?"

Meredith nodded. "I get it."

"We had the best neighborhood," continued Rebecca. "It was our version of Camelot. Pretty streets, old houses, trees, gardens, the park in the square. And St. Kieran's was the center of it all. Stuff going on all the time, every season. It didn't matter if your kids went to school there or the public school, we'd all gather for parish events, and stay involved. It was a simpler time, but we felt like we had it all. And I'll tell you, when Tallie and the choir sang or rang those bells, it was just beautiful. Kelvin and I love our new church on the island, but there was something special about that time we all shared."

"I had no idea you were old friends," said Julia. "We stopped to see her this morning, about the missing bells."

"She loved those bells." Rebecca smiled in remembrance. "And she loved Miss Rose. Rose Mulholland was rich, and Tallie lived paycheck-to-paycheck, but they were two peas in a pod. I remember when Miss Rose and Hank dropped those bells off in the music room. Tallie was overwhelmed. She'd always dreamt of starting a bell choir, but the church couldn't afford them. I remember Rose saying that anything that could pay homage to the Lord in such a beautiful way shouldn't be locked in an attic, no matter what secrets they once held."

Meredith jumped on Rebecca's choice of words. "Secrets?" she asked.

She hadn't gotten the word out of her mouth before Julia chimed in. "With the bells?" And one look at Rebecca's face said that what they had suspected all along was true. Those bells meant something to someone. They had a past. A history.

But did that history have anything to do with the theft?

That was the question they needed to answer.

Chapter Twenty-Four

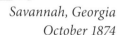

Savannah, Georgia
October 1874

"I hardly know ye, Bridie girl, all grown up like you are."
Brian swagged up his brogue intentionally as Bridie alighted
from the late-afternoon train.

She laughed as she raced across the depot to embrace
him. "I think you know me well enough to take me home and
give me a proper supper, Father. I have spent far too long
studying and working. The thought of a meal made by someone else is most alluring. You got my wire?"

She spoke so well.

His heart swelled to hear it, that this precious girl, a baby
threatened merely by her relationship to a powerful family, was
now an accomplished woman. An accomplished American
woman, he corrected himself, and the pride he felt in that was
dear. "I'm here, so I must have, but if you're referencing the
idea of staying north and working there, Bridie, I just don't
know." He gripped her shoulders. "Your ma isn't well, girl.
She's not been well for a bit, but she wouldn't have me tell

you, although I would have said as much if you hadn't come home now. Because you need to know."

Concern quickly replaced her happy smile. "It's that bad, Da?"

It was. He nodded.

"Take me to her. I can wait to work up North and I can set my own schedule. But I'm not certain how folks here will accept a woman doctor even though I managed to come in first in my class and the hospital loved me."

"Miss Bridie!" A familiar friendly voice haled Bridget from across the raised platform.

"Blue!" Bridie crossed to the man's side and gave him a hug. Brian wasn't sure if her actions sprang from a spontaneous nature or his girl's tough-edged demeanor that didn't care what others might think. Ever. And yet she was so good and hardworking that no one could get much upset. "Have you been keeping an eye on me ma and da, sir?"

Brian read the trouble in Blue's gaze, and Bridie was smart. She'd see it too. Blue understood Mary Kate's timeline, but he played along. "I have, and they've done well. It's an amazing head for business your father has, Bridie Mulholland. It's stood him well in many ways."

"He had the courage to cross over when our future in Ireland dimmed." She sent her father a fond smile. "He set the bar high for his family."

"And provided well," said Blue with a teasing grin. Then he clapped a hand over his mouth when he noted Brian's look of warning. Moving to the grand house was a surprise.

"A secret, eh?" Bridie teased the older man, but she didn't press him too much. "Well, I love a good surprise. And food, Da."

That was the second time she'd mentioned hunger. Once was normal. Twice wasn't. Not for Bridie. She wasn't afraid to build her character and nature by denying herself of this, that, and the other thing, but the thought of one of his kids going hungry wasn't a notion he cared to ponder. "Let's get you home. Supper will be waiting. Blue, you're welcome to join us." He'd made the invitation several times before, and each time Blue had politely declined. Folks had accepted that the mill now had four African American workers. But Blue wasn't foolish enough to let down his guard. Keeping company with white folks could put a target on his back if things turned sour, and Blue was no one's fool. Things could go bad in the blink of an eye.

"Miss Honey has our supper laid by, but I thank you both for the kindly invitation." Blue tipped his cap and grinned at Bridie again. "Mercy, it's good to have you home, Miss Bridie. You are a sight for sore eyes."

"It's good to be back, Blue. And done with school and training," she added.

They hadn't gone far in the wagon when Bridie perked up. "What's this?" she asked when her father directed the wagon toward Harris Street. "We're not going to the farm?"

"Dixie and John Michael Mulholland are running the farm right now."

She looked at him. Really looked. And then she swallowed hard. "It's easier for Mama to be close to things."

"Much. And she'd always dreamed about living in a grand house one day. It wasn't the grandness that drew her, Bridie, it was the room. Space enough to have kids and grandkids and a dog or two, she always said. You'll find her much changed from last year, Daughter."

"Then I'll not waste a bit of our time together," Bridie whispered. She didn't cry.

He knew his girl. She'd save her tears for the privacy of her room. For now she'd put on a firm face for her mother's sake. "Can ye stay long?"

"Oh, Da." She turned and laid that smile on him, and a thing of beauty it was. "I can stay as long as I need, for my skills are sharp and my brain is keen. My job up North will be there. And more alongside, I expect. There's a fever there, Da." She gazed around the seaport city as if assessing. "Different from down here. They want progress there, progress for women, and they want it quickly, although some would say it should have happened long ago. There is little contentment in waiting. I've told them I'll help when I return."

He frowned, confused.

"For the vote, Da. For women. If intelligent women gather around and keep up the conversation, eventually someone will hear. I've been writing to women in New York."

"The Anthony woman."

"And her friend Elizabeth Stanton. They set a tone, Da. A new one, one that must be heard by all. Freedom for all, not some. And the vote for all as well."

His heart claimed a mix of sadness and pride.

She would be a voice to reckon with. He knew that. And he knew why. It was born in her blood to stand tall and speak well, but the North would be claiming another Mulholland soon. Yet who was he to thwart destiny?

He directed the wagon into the carriage house area. Bridie didn't wait for him to come around and help her down. She jumped from the wagon and with a swish of skirts headed inside. When he'd finished with the horses and put things right in the back, he followed her in.

He knew enough to see her rich heritage in her face, in her actions, her drive, and her zeal. How it happened, he didn't know, but it was there, the passion to make things better. Make them right. An O'Connell stance for sure.

But she was theirs now.

A Mulholland.

And whatever she did, she'd do it as a Mulholland. He'd kept the story up for over two decades, and no one questioned it. Nor would they. Because he and Mary Kate never gave them reason to.

Daniel O'Connell's granddaughter would make her mark on America as Bridget Mary Mulholland, and that was fine by him.

Chapter Twenty-Five

"THOSE WERE ROSE'S EXACT WORDS," said Rebecca. "She wasn't one to speak lightly. From the looks on your faces I wish I'd asked more. Or listened more, but I didn't."

"But Hank was with her. You're sure?"

Rebecca nodded. "Hank was always one to be counted on. From the time he was little. I've got to get back," she finished with a quick wave. "I'm doing the afternoon shift and then we're closed for the holiday, but I wanted to make sure you got the cookies."

Meredith sent her an air hug. "It's not that I don't love you, but I don't want the flu for Christmas. No offense, my friend."

Rebecca laughed. "None taken. See you all after the holidays. Merry Christmas!"

"Merry Christmas, Rebecca," said Julia as she pulled out her phone. "And thank you!" She queued up Hank's number and sent a quick text. ARE YOU AVAILABLE FOR A COUPLE OF QUESTIONS?

He replied quickly, a nice surprise. YES, IF YOU DON'T MIND HELPING ME WRAP A GUITAR. I'M AT HOME.

ON OUR WAY.

"Carmen, can you save the sandwiches?" asked Julia.

"Already did. But I won't vouch for the number of cookies that may go missing in your absence. Wow, these are good," she said. "You girls should take one for the road."

Julia didn't have to be coaxed. She grabbed two cookies. So did Meredith. When they pulled up near the Mulholland family home, she appreciated the beautiful wreaths adorning the double door, and the real garland lining the stair rail. There was also feathery green garland beneath the front-facing windows. The entire effect was Home-Sweet-Home, and when she noticed the beautiful Nativity figures framed by the neatly trimmed bushes, she smiled.

Hank let them in a few moments later and led them to an informal sitting room adjacent to the front entry. An early edition of the newspaper was splayed across one chair, and two sets of socks and slippers were tossed not far from cozy chairs. "Clearly we live here," he said. "Amanda would scold me for not putting things right before you arrived, but I've got to get these things wrapped before Hank Jr. gets home at six. Fortunately for me reinforcements arrived in the nick of time." He grinned at the young woman struggling with an odd-shaped container on a good-sized side table. "My daughter Rory, home for the holidays from Emory. This is Mrs. Bellefontaine and Judge Foley."

Julia didn't mention they knew where Rory went to school, and Meredith used Chase as an ice breaker. "My son Chase teaches there. He's a history professor. Are you required to take any history courses as an undergrad?"

Rory maneuvered a piece of tape into place to hold the paper down before she answered. "My freshman year, yes ma'am, but I'm in the accelerated PA program and they don't make us take too many classes outside our major. But I know who he is, ma'am." She flashed a grin Meredith's way. "Plenty of the girls have crushes on him. It would be cute if it wasn't so high-school-ish. He seems oblivious though."

Meredith burst out laughing. "That's Chase all right. I tease him about it whenever he's home. So Hank, can we ask you a couple of questions about those bells if we help wrap?"

"The price sounds right to me." He winked at Rory. "Rory's about to head out for some girl time with friends, so I'll take all the help I can get. She used to play those bells, did you know that?"

Meredith and Julia both shook their heads.

"The adult choir played for one service and the youth choir played at others, and there was always an argument about who would sing and play for Christmas Eve. Finally Tallie solved that by having the youth choir play at the evening service and the adult choir play at the midnight service. That smoothed some ruffled feathers."

"Rory, that's wonderful."

Rory flashed an inviting smile. "We loved playing the bells. I was in elementary school at the time and couldn't sing a note, but I could ring a bell, and Miss Tallie made us all feel like we were important. And it *felt* important, to be up there, in front of the congregation, making pretty music."

Hank agreed, clearly proud. "Tallie had a knack with the kids. They loved her. She loved them. It was a special time, and Grandma would sit there in the middle of that old church and listen to those bells being rung and smile. We didn't have her for much longer after that, but she was so happy to see one of her own playing the bells."

"That was a long time ago, Dad."

"And a memory your grandmother never forgot."

"What's first?" asked Meredith, indicating the wrapping table.

He motioned to a set of football shoulder pads, and as Meredith moved forward, Rory's phone buzzed. She glanced down. Her expression changed. She righted it again quickly, but it was just enough to pique Julia's curiosity.

Meredith held the paper down while Hank tore off pieces of tape. "A friend of ours remembers you and your grandmother dropping them off at the church all those years ago. She said you were quite young."

"I remember it well. My grandma was one of the best women I've ever known, and she was fit to be tied that day. She'd had a run-in with Fiona and her mother and Uncle Will because none of them were planning on attending the Christmas services. I believe Uncle Will called it unessential, and Fee referred to church as useless. All of which angered my grandmother because she wasn't just a woman of faith. Rose Mulholland was a woman of action. She called it faith in action. Remember that, Rory?"

"I do."

She said the words, but her smile had faded, and Julia understood. Remembering lost loved ones was always especially hard during the holidays. Rory lifted the finished package and carried it off toward the back of the house.

"Anyway, she had me go up to the attic with her. The attic isn't nearly as crowded now. We've gone through a lot of the things that were there and sorted them out. We donated some things. Tossed others." He winced when he admitted that. "I could almost feel Grandma watching me make those decisions of what to keep and what to throw out, because she treated that attic with such respect.

'Your history is here, within these walls,' she'd tell us, but I think only one or two of us ever listened. Anyway, we carried the bells downstairs, put them in the car, and drove them over to the church while they were having choir practice. My grandma couldn't carry a tune, but she loved music, and she loved God, and she wanted Miss Tallie to have those bells, so Miss Tallie was understandably hurt when they were donated to the museum. She argued with Reverend Martin for days, but Grandma was fighting a losing battle with cancer, much like Tallie is now, and I had to tell her to leave it alone because the bells weren't ours any longer. We had to respect his choices. I did pay him a visit later and told him in no uncertain terms how he'd hurt my grandmother and that he needn't expect our monthly donation from that point on."

"How did he take that?" asked Julia.

"He was kind of dumbfounded at first, as if he hadn't expected repercussions. Then he got upset, but almost more at himself than me. It was odd. I wasn't doing it for revenge. It just made no sense to support a church that none of us were attending any longer. Grandma and Amanda and I were going to a different church and offering our support there. The rest of the family had pretty much shrugged off church. Some have come back now," he added. "That would please Grandma. But I won't pretend I wasn't angry when he gave the bells away, because it upset Grandma. And I'd have done anything to keep from upsetting her."

"The pastor sold them, Hank." Meredith was miffed and didn't hide it. "He didn't give them away. He sold them to the museum and never told a soul about it. We went to see him about it, but he wasn't at the church."

"Sold them? Really?" Hank frowned. "I suppose I shouldn't be surprised. Maybe that's why he looked like he was second-guessing himself when I stopped our offering. We were always quite generous with the church. If he lost a significant annual offering because he sold the bells, that would be a hard knock when you're running a shrinking congregation. But I'm surprised that I didn't hear about the sale. We had family friends working at St. Kieran's until nine or ten years ago. It would have to show up in the accounting, wouldn't it?"

Meredith and Julia exchanged looks. "I don't know that it would, necessarily," said Julia.

"Oh man." Hank ran his hand through his hair. He had that wavy, thick Irish hair that never seemed to thin. "You think he might have taken the money for himself? That's a scandal that could cost him his job."

"I heard he's retiring at the end of the year," said Julia.

"Well, it could cost his retirement too. That's a felony, to misappropriate funds like that, at least if they're above a certain threshold."

"He was paid over twenty-thousand dollars, according to the museum."

Hank's brows knit together. "Definitely a felony, although past the statute of limitations most likely. Still, things like this have serious repercussions besides possible incarceration and payback. He could lose his retirement benefits."

"I hadn't thought of that."

Hank and Meredith finished the final side of the awkwardly shaped set of shoulder pads. He blew out a puff of air as Rory came back into the room. She'd looked happy when they first arrived. Now she seemed restive.

"I don't expect he considered these consequences when he sold them. And while the time frame probably erases a criminal pursuit, the church isn't bound by that to stop his benefits. He could have a lot to lose, ladies, and folks with a lot to lose aren't always trustworthy. I've noticed he doesn't like being backed into a corner, and he's not afraid to stand his ground."

A corner.

The bells.

And who would stand to gain the most?

Julia set the tape down quickly as things clicked into place in her brain. Suddenly she could see who stood to gain by the theft of the bells, and it wasn't the pastor. "Mere. We've got to go."

Meredith didn't miss a beat, which was why they worked so well together. She'd go along with whatever Julia said, even if she didn't have a clue why they were doing it. "Oh, that's right," she said. "We've got to head out. Hank." She turned to him before they left. "There's something hidden about those bells. I don't know what. I don't know how they're tied into your family, but I've searched the historic records, and I know that the story about buying them from circus performers isn't true. I have proof. But your grandmother mentioned secrets attached to the bells when she gave them to St. Kieran's."

"I'd forgotten that, but yes. Yes, she did."

"See what you can find out," Meredith told him. "If anyone kept a journal or a diary or anything from those early Mulhollands that might give us a lead, that would be helpful. I'm not sure if the secret your grandmother was referring to has anything to do with the theft, but it could, and we don't dare rule anything out."

"I understand. I know you said your neighbor has been questioned by the police." He aimed a sympathetic look at Julia. "That's never a comfortable place to be."

"It's not, and she's a single mom with two kids. I know she didn't do it, but I have this fear of seeing her locked up for Christmas. Everything points to her. And yet I'm 100 percent certain she's innocent."

"I'll look in the attic to see if there's anything I can unearth," Hank promised. "As soon as I've put this stuff away."

"Thank you. And just so you know, you got my vote last time. And you'll get it again," Julia promised him.

"Mine too," Meredith assured him. "Nice meeting you, Rory."

"Oh, yes. Nice. Very nice." Rory gave them an almost pained smile. She went one way.

They went the other.

"Where are we going?" asked Meredith as they hurried down the block to the car.

"Tallie's."

"Tallie's?"

"Yes." Julia put the car into drive, signaled, and pulled out into traffic. "I see it all now, Mere. The whole thing, and it seems so obvious that I don't know how we didn't figure it out sooner. I can't believe my mind never even went to it. Not for a minute."

Meredith had turned in her seat. "Went to what?"

"Altruism at its finest," Julia said softly. "A Christmas wish fulfilled by the very people we'd suspect the least. If I'm right, Rory Webster isn't hurrying off to some holiday party time with the girls. She's heading to bell choir practice."

Chapter Twenty-Six

MEREDITH TEXTED CARMEN ABOUT WHAT they were doing. They pulled into Tallie's driveway twenty-two minutes later.

"Julia. There's a gray sedan parked in that stand of trees."

A chill raced down Julia's spine as they turned in to Tallie's driveway. Was it Reverend Martin's gray car? If her theory was correct, what was he doing here?

The car was nudged nose-first into the tree line west of Tallie's driveway. But a few hundred feet away, where the pretty barn stood at the end of the broad, graveled driveway, were half a dozen cars, and the lights of the barn were on.

Was the reverend over there? Then why park here, hidden in the thick copse of trees?

No house lights glowed from within. Only a front light, over the stoop, broke the darkness. The house looked quiet and empty. No TV flicker danced off the windowpanes, and no one had turned on the outdoor Christmas lights. The little house stood starkly alone. Julia pulled off the drive and parked behind the gray car. There was no way to completely block it in, but they could make it a little bit harder for whoever it was to beat a hasty retreat. They both climbed out.

"Check that car, Mere."

Julia whispered the words, and Meredith circled the hidden gray car, peering. "Empty," she whispered back.

They hunched low and snuck up the drive, to the front of the house.

Julia checked the door.

Locked. She crept across the grass in front of the thinning bushes and then around back.

Still nothing. No one. And not a sound—

The light smash of tinkling glass pierced the air. Within seconds, a few other sounds of shattering joined in, and then the quiet sound of a door latch cut the quiet. And then nothing.

"He's broken the window on the back door of her garage," whispered Meredith. "Old single-pane glass. It's the only kind that breaks that easily."

"But why is the parish priest breaking into Tallie's house?" Julia whispered back. "What's in there?"

"No clue."

Tallie had left a night-light on in the kitchen. A shadow crept past the light. Julia ducked then exchanged a sheepish look with Meredith. "We can see him," Julia whispered.

"But he can't see us. Duh," Meredith whispered back. "Should we go wait by his car? Confront him there?"

"That could risk Tallie getting home and walking in on him."

"We stand guard out here?"

"But what is he doing in there? Looking for the bells? Robbing her?" Julia made a face. "I'm not sure what to do."

"How about if you both turn around and walk yourselves over to that handy little shed?" growled a voice right behind them.

Julia's heart stopped then sped up as she turned around, and she was sure Meredith had a similar adrenaline rush.

"I didn't spend ten years planning a peaceful retirement to have the two of you mess it up for me."

Julia switched her phone light on, but it wasn't Reverend Martin standing there. It was Hopkins, the groundskeeper. The last person she expected to see.

"What are you talking about?" Meredith asked. "What is it that you've actually done? We know you didn't steal the bells."

"Stupid bells. The sound drove the pastor crazy. I told him we could make a donation of them way back when, and he thought that was a good idea. Giving them away would mean he didn't have to hear them anymore. He's not a bad guy, but he's not real strong, which left me a lot more work than I used to have. Fewer volunteers, more work, no raise. Not what anyone looks for, now is it? And no one is eager to hire a fiftysomething groundskeeper and handyman anymore. Most places hire services to just come in and do it for them. But they weren't about to pay me what I was making after thirty-five years of working that parish building and grounds, keeping things running."

"The reverend didn't know you got a tidy sum for them." Julia saw something in his hand but wasn't sure what. A gun? A knife? Or was he bluffing?

"No reason to tell him," said Hopkins. "Turn around." He poked Meredith in the back to move them along. "Get on, there. Hurry it up. I don't have all night. That little shed out back looks like the best place to put the pair of you. By the time anyone hears you, I'll be long gone. Then who cares?"

"You're on limited time because we have a friend about to arrive," Julia told him. She stopped walking. "And when she sees your car, she'll realize we've run into trouble."

"Blah, blah, blah." He drew closer to Julia. "You think I'm going to believe that? Just because you happened to show up while I was looking for her stash? Stupid old lady hid it where all old ladies hide things, in her underwear drawer."

"But why take Tallie's money?"

"That choir cost me a lot of late nights. People tromping in three days a week, wet boots and shoes. Practicing over and over again, same stuff, same way. And I had to stay until their practices were done, which meant when the yammer mouths stopped talking. And they never stopped talking."

"So they made you a lot of extra work." Julia was trying to see what he held without letting him know she was trying to see it.

"Wasn't she nice to you?" asked Meredith.

He prodded her again, pushing her backward, and Julia was pretty sure he held some kind of pipe. But she wasn't absolutely certain.

A pipe was dangerous, but not as dangerous as a gun.

"Nice would have been letting me get home to bed before ten o'clock three nights a week. If Martin had given her a key, that would have been different, but he only let me and Myrna have keys. That meant I had to be there to lock up."

"He trusted you."

"Used me is how I see it," Hopkins replied. "But I figured out how to get the pay I was due. The bells went to the museum, and then this and that got sold here and there. With so many folks leaving, nobody noticed things went missing. Reverend Mix had given me access to one of the accounts for upkeep and repairs, so me plugging in a church check and taking money out for expenses wasn't anything unusual."

"You don't feel bad about betraying that trust?" asked Julia as she tried to figure out how to get them out of this.

"Walk." He directed them with a wave toward the back fence.

That one movement confirmed her suspicions. Pipe, not gun.

A car put on a signal light out on the road. She jerked her head that way. "That should be Carmen."

Hopkins snorted disbelief. He didn't turn, not until the lights of the car began to come up the driveway, toward the house. His gaze darted left. He glanced back over his shoulder. The sight of the moving lights made him hesitate, giving Julia just enough time to hit 911 on her phone.

He whirled back. Saw the phone. Raised his arm. And the look on his face, a look of anger snarled with frustration, was almost more frightening than the pipe. For a moment, she thought the angry man was going to make it a test of wills.

"911. Please state your emergency."

Meredith yelled out the address.

Hopkins swung the pipe.

Meredith bobbed.

Julia weaved. The phone went flying, and the pipe caught nothing else but air as Carmen's lights flooded the front yard.

Hopkins glared at Julia.

Then at Meredith.

Then he dropped the pipe and raced toward the front of the house.

"I'll tell dispatch what's going on," said Meredith, pulling out her phone.

Julia left Meredith to make the call and chased after Hopkins. If he made it to his car, he'd have to drive hundreds of feet forward through the thick trees, if that was even possible, because she'd parked directly behind him. But as they neared the front of the house and Carmen's car, two things happened simultaneously.

Carmen reached out a long-handled something and whacked Hopkins's legs right out from under him, dropping him to the ground as the barn door swung open wide.

And then music filled the air.

Beautiful, heart-grabbing music, the kind that fuels the heart and feeds the soul, a hauntingly beautiful rendition of "Silent Night," played so uniquely that Julia knew she'd never hear that beautiful hymn again as sweetly as she did this night because here, in Tallie O'Meara's barn, they'd found the bells.

***

"What's going on?" A familiar young woman raced toward Julia and Carmen. She spotted the handyman on the ground and stopped dead. "Where's Tallie? What's happening?"

"Where's Tallie supposed to be?" asked Julia, but she never took her eyes off Hopkins on the ground.

"She and a couple of friends were going to see *A Christmas Carol* near the waterfront. It's an annual thing and they make a night of it."

"Leaving the perfect time for one final practice, I expect." Meredith came up alongside. "You're Tallie's granddaughter, aren't you?"

"Yes."

"And you were there to help hand out pastries the day the bells went missing."

"The day the bells were borrowed," the young woman insisted. "We have every intention of giving them back once Grandma hears them played again."

"One last time," said Meredith, and the young woman nodded. Flashing lights and a siren indicated the sheriff's swift approach. "You might want to get back inside, honey. Let the officers do their thing. And then we'll talk about those bells."

Tallie's granddaughter hesitated but then took Meredith's advice. She dashed back into the barn and slid the door shut as the police cruisers pulled into the driveway.

The deputies hurried to the women, and after they were interviewed, three things were clear: Hopkins wouldn't be making his flight to the land of easy retirement, Tasha would be declared innocent, and Tallie's money would be returned once it had been released from evidence.

In the meantime, they had to figure out a way for the young choir to play those bells for the Christmas Eve service so Tallie O'Meara would hear them, with all the sparkling clarity and tone she loved…one last time.

Chapter Twenty-Seven

JULIA HAD SAID SHE DIDN'T want to work Christmas Eve, but this time there was no choice, so here they were, a critical meeting of the minds in the spacious conference room. The museum's director and associate director were both there. So were Tallie's granddaughters, Emmie and Lauren. Reverend Martin was there too, along with Hank Webster and his daughter Rory. The girls had been brought into the stationhouse for questioning two days before, but Detective Lansing had agreed to a meeting here, today, and that was a nice thing for the stone-faced detective to do.

Carmen had brought in extra chairs.

The coffeepot was full with a backup decanter on the table. Meredith had turned the gas fireplace on, and its cheerful glow helped soften the meeting's focus. It was Christmas Eve, after all. But before anything else was decided, Lauren and Emmie O'Meara and Rory Webster had a separate meeting to go to.

Meredith took the girls into Julia's office and closed the door with a quiet click.

Jay and Tasha were seated there. They stood when the girls came in.

Emmie took one look at Tasha and started crying. Lauren didn't, but her eyes grew moist and her chin quivered. Rory drew a breath.

"We messed up big-time," she said softly. She faced Tasha. "When we talked about this, we never looked beyond taking the bells and smuggling them out. It was for a good cause, so we never thought about hurting others."

"Or you getting blamed," said Emmie. Meredith handed her tissues, and she didn't carefully dab her eyes. She swiped them roundly and blew her nose. "We were stupid for not even considering that, and we're supposed to be smart. I'm sorry, Tasha. You hired us and trusted us, and we messed up."

"Can you forgive us?" Lauren might not be crying, but she looked forlorn. "Our intent was good, but our execution had some major flaws."

Tasha folded her arms across her chest. "Would you do it again?"

Rory shook her head. "No. We'd figure out another way to honor Miss Tallie. We didn't think about how it would hurt both of you. Miss Tallie is dying." She took a deep breath. "We know how hurt she was when the choir disbanded and the bells were given away. It broke my great-grandmother's heart," she explained in a voice rife with emotion. "There was nothing we could do because she'd given away her rights when she donated the bells. She never thought they might be given away. It made her sad in her final months, and I just wanted Miss Tallie to feel some of the joy she used to feel. The joy she gave to so many others with her choir music and her bells. I'm truly sorry." She took another deep breath. "I've disappointed my parents and myself, and I know we all feel the same way."

Jay and Tasha exchanged looks, and then Tasha spoke. "I forgive you." Her voice was soft. "I lost my grandmother this past year, and it broke my heart to say goodbye. If I could have made her final days easier, I'd have done it, but there was nothing to do. So I understand your motives. Not your actions." She added the last in a firmer voice. "You took advantage of my trust in you, and if you'd pleaded your case to me about the bells, I could have asked my boss to lift the secure requirement on the bells. We've done that a few times in the past."

"You have?" The three girls exchanged expressions of surprise. "Really?"

"We don't brag about it or advertise it, because it can't become a common thing, but yes. We're people. With hearts." Tasha sighed. "I would have pleaded your case, and all of this could have been avoided."

"Unbelievable." Lauren tipped her head back then sighed. "We're dumb. And sorry. And I'm really sorry we messed up your December when it should have been nice. For both of you," she added with a glance toward Jay.

"What do you say, Tasha?" Jay looked gruff, but Julia read the compassion behind his stern gaze.

"I say we all wish one another a Merry Christmas and go home to our families."

"I'm down with that." He faced the girls. "I hope they go easy on you, but not too easy, because it's been a rough month. But after losing my mother this year, following a long battle with cancer, I can honestly say I understand. Merry Christmas."

"Merry Christmas." They left quietly. On her way out, though, Tasha turned back toward Julia. She sent her a smile of gratitude. Julia returned the look, and then she and Meredith took the three girls down to the conference room for another reckoning.

Detective Lansing was the last person to arrive. He nailed Julia with a hard-edged look as he came through the front door. "Generally my meetings with felons take place at the station house."

"And generally your accused aren't beloved granddaughters and their musical friends trying to make a dying woman's last Christmas special." She kept her tone soft. "That makes this case unique, and I think given the day and the hour and the fact that we all want to go home and celebrate Christ's birth, we can make this quick and easy."

He didn't frown, but he didn't seem convinced either. And yet he was here, and that counted for something.

Julia let him lead the way into the room.

Everyone sat straighter, seeing him. Except Hank. He stood, rounded the table, clasped Lansing's hand, and said, "Good. You've come to throw the book at the miscreants and about time too. Don't forget to nab my firstborn in the sting, Detective." Rory couldn't see her father's smile. Julia could and had to bite back one of her own. "It'll look bad for reelection, but I might be able to spin it to my favor when all is said and done."

"I've got officers waiting with handcuffs, Councilman."

"So be it."

Hank returned to his seat, and once they were all seated, with Carmen keeping an eye on the door and the coffee service, Julia began. "I've presided over a lot of convoluted cases in my time, but this one has been singularly unique for Meredith and me. We didn't have just one case going on. We had two, and until we recognized that, the layers were interwoven. It took some serious unraveling, but we've gotten to this point, so that's good. The purpose of this meeting is twofold." She locked eyes with the museum director.

"First, to see if we can reduce the charges against the girls for taking the bells. I argue this for two reasons," she added. "One, the altruistic nature of their mission, to have a bell choir accompany Christmas services for their dying grandmother, granting her one last Christmas wish before she hears a more heavenly choir."

Was she laying it on a little thick?

Yes. Purposely. Because she really loved what these young women were willing to do to make an old woman happy.

"And second, because their purpose was for no personal gain, I would argue as a former judge that there's no need to have a record attached to their good names. Having said this, we recognize that their actions caused considerable angst and suffering on the part of some museum staff. For that I would suggest some sort of reparation on the part of the young women involved. Gina? What do you think?"

The museum's associate director folded her hands and made eye contact with the three young women. "Judge Foley is right. Your actions created an atmosphere of suspicion and intolerance between the museum workers. Ms. Alexander has been in fear for her job and questioned multiple times by police. Our security guard has been worried that the Savannah Police might withdraw their invitation for him to join the academy next month. They were both deeply affected by your rash actions."

"I'm sorry. We're all sorry about that." Emmie leaned forward. "I can speak for all of us when I say we're so sorry for the angst and division we caused. That was never our intent." She exchanged looks with Rory and Lauren. They both nodded. "We just wanted to make Gran's last Christmas special, and there are no available bells any-where. We checked. You can even check our online searches," she assured the director and the stone-faced detective. "We'd have borrowed them if we could have, but the museum has a firm 'no borrow' policy on things left unsecured, and we knew we couldn't secure a place and meet that policy. Not and keep the secret. So we're sorry. Truly sorry." She faced the director. "We didn't think anyone would suspect someone at the museum, because you're all good people, but when we got the job to serve food, Tasha had everyone do a practice run the week before. We heard Jay and Tasha going over the protocol. She explained to Jay that the bell case would be unlocked so Rory's dad could have a photo op, and we realized we had the perfect storm. We had pastry carts, an open bell case, and Gran's barn. Gran hasn't gone into that barn in over twenty years—she's afraid of mice—but my uncle used to use it for his rock band in the eighties. It's got this music-friendly corner that Great-Grandpa soundproofed because he hated rock music. That made the perfect practice site."

"But were you able to get everyone together to practice in the barn enough times?" asked Meredith.

"We did virtual practice," Rory explained. "We sent the music to everyone. They all had bell assignments. All they had to do was practice the timing on Zoom calls as if they were actually lifting and ringing the bells. It worked, because we sounded marvelous on Tuesday night." She raised an eyebrow and scanned the group. "If you allow us to do this…" She leaned forward slightly, and her convincing plea showed her Hank Mulholland Webster lineage. "It'll mean so much to Miss Tallie. We all love her. We just wanted to tell her that with one last Christmas filled with the bells she and my great-grandmother loved so much."

"But how did you get the electricity shut off?" queried Meredith. "That had to be part of the plan."

Lauren raised her hand. "My cousin's fiancé told us how to shut down electric if we ever needed to. We didn't tell him why we were asking," she assured the group. "He explained how circuit breakers work and how construction crews run things differently so they don't trip them, so all we had to do was shut one down. They're labeled, so it wasn't even difficult," she admitted.

"There aren't any locks on the panel in the basement, and everyone assumed the construction caused the problem. By the time they figured out it was a tripped circuit, we had the bells in the car and were back upstairs. What we didn't expect were protesters." Lauren exchanged a rueful look with Hank. "We couldn't believe all those people came there to yell about stuff when you were doing such a good thing, but it created an even bigger distraction for us."

"So inadvertently helped your cause."

"Yes. Sorry." She looked genuinely glum. "We all felt awful about that."

"Councilman, I'm curious as to why you didn't recognize these young ladies at the event," said Lansing. "You've known their families for years."

"I never saw them," Hank said. "We didn't cross over to that area prior to my talk, and the view was blocked by some kind of display, so I couldn't see the coffee and pastry area from where I was. If I had, I would have recognized Lauren and Emmie. They're the kind of girls who are always putting forth their best effort, so their presence wouldn't have surprised me. When the lights went out and people began panicking, my campaign people ushered me out in case there was something more sinister going on."

"Of course."

"Did you kidnap my Nativity figurines?" asked Julia.

Lauren nodded, sheepish. "And then we couldn't sleep so we brought them back."

Julia wanted to hug them, but of course they were in deep trouble…for doing something so nice that she couldn't remember the last time someone had put together a plan as good and kind, although somewhat devious as this one. It made her kind of proud to be part of it.

"May I say something?" Reverend Martin raised his hand, and when Julia nodded, he stood. "I need to take my share of the blame," he began. On their first meeting, he'd come across as rather dismissive. Today he seemed more personable.

"I'm not a born leader," he told them. "I never have been. I entered ministry to do ecclesiastical work because it suited me. I write things. I edit things. I'm a biblical scholar, and that's my comfort zone. When I was called to take over for Reverend Mix, my pledge of obedience required me to say yes. In retrospect I probably should have said no. I haven't done as well as I could have. My hearing sensitivities made singing and bells a torment, but instead of admitting that was the problem, I distanced myself from my parishioners. If I'd handled all of that better, I might have been able to be Jerry Hopkins's friend and not just his priest. And if I hadn't given him so many extra duties, or if I'd fought harder for a raise for him, he might not have grown so resentful. I might be a man of God, but I'm frighteningly human, and I want to own my responsibility here. And to offer this in apology." He motioned toward Lauren, Emmie, and Rory. "If the young ladies are kept out of jail for the Christmas Eve service, I'd like to host it at St. Kieran's. And I'd like to invite Father Mix and some others to come join us. I'm just sorry it took something like this for me to see my own short-comings and pride. I should have known better."

"Really?" Emmie stared at him, and there was no mistaking the new hope in her eyes. Her brows shot up. "You'd do that for us?"

"It would be an honor."

Before the room got a little misty, Detective Lansing cleared his throat. "Just a minute, here."

His words made the entire room pause.

"Am I to understand that you're all in agreement that I let these three go free, and all who aided and/or abetted their mission, gather together at church tonight, and go about our holiday as if this were all okay?"

Meredith cheered. "Detective, what a marvelous idea! A number-one idea. Surely the best that could be expected."

Lansing leveled a look at her. Then Julia. Then the girls. "You will do community service. All three of you. You will work at home-less shelters while you're home on Christmas break, beginning tomorrow on Christmas Day. Do you understand me?"

Hope widened the three young women's eyes while anticipation softened their faces. "Really? We can play the bells tonight and help tomorrow?" It was Emmie who spoke. "And then we'll give the bells back on the twenty-sixth."

"And I will check with the shelter each and every day, ladies. Don't think for a moment I won't."

"Yes, sir." All three young women nodded, and there was no denying the relief in their faces.

"Well, something else has come up about the bells, but it's nothing that concerns the good detective," said Hank. "Detective, if it's agreeable to you, the girls will show up at the Old City Mission first thing tomorrow."

"Nine o'clock. Sharp."

All three girls nodded. Their relief was palpable.

Lansing let himself out, and Julia turned back to Hank. He reached into his jacket pocket and withdrew a yellowed page. The shade of paper and the curving script gave it a vintage look. The formation of cursive letters flowed like an old-world document. He unfolded the letter and made a show of holding it high. And then he read it aloud.

Brian—

Here they are, a down payment as promised, despite your refusal, for one never knows when times may grow hard and harsh. Something put by is always welcome, even as assurance against a claim.

I knew ye would agree, for such a one are ye, sir. A friend of honor. A champion. One who would never let an innocent babe become the target of ill will, no matter what family crest she bears.

I know ye refused payment in kind, but if the sale of these bells brings needed cash during hard times, so be it. They were from a grander church up north, gifted by a man with much to lose and so came to me for the assurance of Bridie's well-being, knowing his claim would be her ruination. And likely her demise.

A new venture in a new land has its own pitfalls. These will help see that all goes well, both with the child and my soul. Her family knows nothing of this. They are of the belief that someone has dispatched her as directed by her uncles. That such is not the case, will never be told to the O'Connells. It is our secret, and only ours, and ever will be. God's peace.

S.

Meredith stared at him. "But what does that mean? What secret has been kept?"

"A child." Julia whispered the words and held Hank's gaze. "They saved a child."

"And not just any child," noted Hank. He withdrew a few old, folded documents. "Bridget Mary Mulholland, the illegitimate granddaughter of the famous Irish orator and member of Parliament, Daniel O'Connell."

Meredith's jaw dropped open.

Hank held up a birth certificate. "Our Bridie, the woman who became one of the first female doctors to practice, the abolitionist and suffragist, the woman who helped save lives here in Savannah and up North, was sent into hiding to save her life because rumors of infidelity were plaguing the O'Connell family. Her mother gave her away to save her life."

Sacrificial love.

The very best part of a wonderful Christmas.

Julia looked at Meredith. "Well, I know we didn't want to work on Christmas Eve, but this." She swept the room full of people a look of compassion and joy. "This has to be the best Christmas ever."

And that night, at little St. Kieran's church, it wasn't just a handful of people and Hank Webster's family that showed up to hear the bells ring Christmas Day in.

The entire Mulholland clan came.

And there was no fighting, no squabbling, no fussing, and no fuming.

For this day—

And this night—

They were one.

Chapter Twenty-Eight

The grand house felt worn.

It wasn't worn.

He was.

Brian thought he'd been ready to give his beloved wife and partner a farewell kiss as the New Year approached, but he was sorely mistaken. He wasn't one bit ready.

Who could be? Not when she'd shared not only his life and his bed but his goals, his dreams, his business. She'd made his business her own with those fine laces and new opportunities for women. So maybe Bridie didn't get all her gifts from nature. Maybe nature was augmented by her mother's fine, strong example.

Bridie came through the hallway just then. Her cloak was wet. She slung it onto a hook near the kitchen fire and worked off her boots with a grimace. "There will be a day when women can work and wear sensible shoes that do not require a Congressional motion to remove them from one's feet. Bah." She wriggled her second foot out and stood the boots alongside the fire, not far from his. "Is it odd that with a big, lovely home, you and I find ourselves in this kitchen more often than not, Da? And Lorna has left soup and bread, a perfect combination on a cold, wet Georgia day. Have you eaten, Father?"

Her linguistics danced back and forth. She sounded fully American when she addressed a group of people as she had in the old hall a week past, or she could go fully Irish with a lilting brogue that rivaled her mother's. "I waited for you."

"But it's late." She motioned to the outdoors. "And though the days are beginning to lengthen, there's still too much dreariness about. I'll ladle our bowls."

He let her do it. And he let her slice the bread. Lorna had left a pot of butter on the table. It was good butter, sweet and mild with none of the tang of whey that careless handling brought forth. Lorna knew he liked soft butter. Nothing to fight the bread.

"Here we are."

She set the food down, kissed his cheek, and said grace.

It was time. He knew it. He hated it. But it was time. "You need to go back north, darlin' girl."

She made a face and started to wave him off, but he stood firm. "You know it's time, Bridie. It's not that I don't appreciate the help and the love, but your mother would skin me alive, and be right to do so, if she thought I'd let you squander years of study and aptitude on taking care of me when I have no need. I'm fit. I'm capable."

"But lonely."

"Aye, there's that, and it's unlikely to abate anytime soon. Time heals, they say, and it was true when we lost your brother. It didn't heal the loss, but it stitched up the empty hole after a time."

"Then I'll stay for that time," she said. But he couldn't let her do that. Not knowing what he knew. Not understanding her future. Her talents. Her personal heritage.

"And have your mother's voice scolding me day and night?" He lifted an eyebrow in her direction. "That sounds restful."

"Da."

"I will be fine. I've even talked with your brother and Molly about moving in here. With her expecting again, their family would fill this house with the love and laughter your mother wanted. It will be her dream, fulfilled, and you know she wanted more for you children than she could ever desire for herself."

"I know the truth in that, but Da—"

He reached over and put a hand on hers. "Spring is quick to come. I'll be busy night and day with lambs being born at the farm, with auction, with overseeing the planting and the mill. And I've put John Michael's wife in charge of laces. She's got a fine head for business, whereas his head is more a straight-line sort."

"Ambitious but narrow."

"Yes. But capable as long as the job goes along the path." He pressed her hand lightly. "You've done the right thing, Bridie. Always. But now it's my turn to make sure you're on the right path, and we know that lies elsewhere."

She studied him quietly. Then she nodded, but as she did, she posed a question, a question he was ill prepared to answer. "Da, what about those bells in the attic? Of what use are they? And when did we get them? I've never seen them played or even knew of their existence before I went up to gather some things to give to those in need and found them tucked aside."

He choked on a bit of potato. Those bells had been put away and kept away purposely all this time. He hadn't needed them to pay his daughter's way.

He'd done that himself, and he'd kept the bells. What else was there to do with them?

She got him a glass of water and brought it over quickly. "Smaller bites," she scolded.

He took a long drink, steadied his voice, and nodded. "All is well now. I should have been more careful." He took another sip of water and then told the biggest lie he'd ever told. "Your mother loved the sounds of a bell-ringing group that came through here a while back, and when they put their bells up for sale, I brought them here hoping to start a bell choir someday. At the church, you know. But our church is smallish yet, and so they sit, gathering dust until we have a church big enough to form a bell-ringing troupe."

"Bells for holy services?"

He nodded and shrugged, pleased she didn't delve deeper. "Bells in the towers, why not bells on the altar? You know your mother's keen ear."

"I do indeed. And keen eyes, as well, to watch for children's youthful misdeeds."

He laughed. "A lot of truth there, although yours were minor." Would she accept the change of subject?

He hoped so.

He rarely thought about the bells, except as a moment of pride in how well he'd cared for this wonderful child, this God-given gift. But what of the letter that came with the bells? Was it there, still?

He hurried to the attic once Bridie left for her first call the next morning.

The bell cases had been pulled out. The smudges of dust showed that she'd opened each one, but as he opened the second case, he edged up the velvety surface from the corner and there was the letter, safe and sound.

He tugged it out.

It would do no good to have it found one day, and now that she'd seen the bells, she would never forget their existence. Let her think he'd purchased them from a band of traveling performers. Better that than the truth, that they were provided as insurance to secure her safety and upbringing.

When the church grew in size, as it should do now that the city had regained some of its footing, they could quietly donate the bells and that would end the story.

They were lovely things, yes. He lifted one and rang it softly. The chime resounded in the lofty attic, much as it would in a church. A beautiful sound, one that should be heard.

But not yet.

And maybe not in his lifetime. Such things were not in his hands. Only the good Lord knew the day and the hour.

He'd leave that in God's hands, but he'd leave his wishes known for the bells. The Mulhollands and Monaghans had worked long and hard and prospered greatly. During a war that scourged so many, they had hung on and thrived.

He'd needed no help guarding Bridie's life and no assistance for her needs.

She was theirs from the first day, and that was all anyone ever needed to know.

He took the letter downstairs. He meant to burn it but hesitated at the last minute.

A deed done in haste could be regretted in leisure. He knew the truth in that.

He took the letter and the papers that came along with it, climbed the stairs to the attic, and tucked the letter in the metal safety box they'd hidden away there upon moving in. The box held bits of Ireland, touches of history, letters from his granny, God rest her soul, and a few missives from his sister, mostly complaining.

The fabric of family.

Mary Kate's words. True now and always.

He stood. Sighed. Drew a breath.

And then he went downstairs and on to work like he did every other day but Sunday.

A good life, all told.

Blessed by God, all his days.

And as he passed by the house of Bridie's first appointment, a woman of gentility whose time was soon to come, the sureness of his daughter's wisdom strengthened him.

He'd done his work. Completed his task. Like Simeon of old, he'd seen the fruits of what was meant to be. And despite his tragic losses, he was grateful.

So grateful.

He went on to the mill, greeted the workers, and examined the work for the day. The new tubs were thick with batts and the sweet, greasy smell of lanolin clung to the cool air. Drums turned and combed the washed fleece on the upper level, teasing it into fibers that could be spun. Above that the threads were woven into bolts of finely turned wool, suitable for those of means and the working class.

From field to factory he'd built a business that not only produced wonderful goods, it honored good hearts. In the end, that was all anyone could ask, and if one were to ask him how and why he came to this land and became so successful, he'd have the perfect answer for them.

The work of God's heart done through human hands.

The thought made him smile. He hadn't smiled much these long, cold months, but the sights and sounds of fairly paid labor drew his satisfaction.

He'd come. He'd toiled. He'd labored. And he'd blessed others.

It was enough.

He climbed the stairs and went back to work. Busy hands mended broken hearts, and he was in the position to know the truth in that. It was a truth he'd live until he could work no longer or the good Lord called him home.

And it was a fine life to live, all in all.

A fine life indeed.

Dear Readers,

The idea for this story came to me when I realized I was doing a Christmas mystery! Naturally I wanted it to be extra special because Christmas is that time of year when folks come out of the woodwork to do nice things! I love it! But what I wanted to show in this story is how we have those kinds of people around us and near us, sacrificing for us all the time, and we don't always see it or appreciate it for what it is: sacrificial love. Even in our simple, normal "everyday" lives, there are folks who are living their faith like Tallie O'Meara.

I've known a lot of Tallies in my time. Some are affiliated with churches, some with schools, some are neighbors. Not all embrace religion, but they're not afraid to have faith and be that helping hand in a crisis. I love that dedication and devotion, ungoverned—a quality that is simply part of their being.

I hope you love this story of a set of missing bells, a quarrelsome family, an honest politician, and a sweet old lady whose love makes things shine. While the historical part of the story shows the ultimate sacrifice of a young mother...a mother who banishes her child from the land she was born to in order to save her life.

I loved that premise in Exodus for Moses and in *Willow* for the little princess, Elora Danan, and other great stories of maternal love.

Sending you my very merriest Christmas greetings! God bless you and keep you, and may His face shine upon you as you go about preparing for this beautiful season! With cookies, I hope!

Ruthy

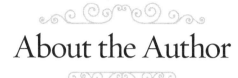

About the Author

USA TODAY BESTSELLING AUTHOR RUTH Logan Herne is living her dream of writing great books and hanging out with really cool people like the editors at Guideposts and the other authors working on these great series. When she replaces her writing hat with a farm hat, Ruthy can be found working on her fifty-acre pumpkin farm in Western New York, a "let's do this for retirement" venture that isn't exactly your typical retirement, but suits Ruthy and Farmer Dave just fine! With over sixty published novels and novellas, Ruthy is enjoying her life as author, speaker, wife, mother, grandmother, baker (and this year, "fried dough maker"!!!!) and plant grower. During the growing season she shares responsibility to raise and display and sell tens of thousands of pumpkins and 2,400 chrysanthemums that get hand-watered and fed daily. She says this keeps her young…and that means she's nimble enough to play and laugh with her fourteen grandkids.

Write to Ruthy at loganherne@gmail.com, friend her on Facebook, and stop by her website. She loves getting to know her readers!

The Truth Behind the Fiction

DANIEL O'CONNELL WASN'T JUST A nineteenth-century Irish political figure. He broke the mold. A learned man who was born in 1775, O'Connell left college because of the French Revolution and went to London to study law. This change gave the young Irishman a whole new perspective. For over twenty years he argued for the rights of Catholics to be able to vote and hold office in Ireland and the UK. His efforts resulted in the Catholic Emancipation Act of 1829 and the opportunity for Irish Catholics to take a vested part in government.

But Daniel and his sons (who followed their father's legacy and into Parliament) tended to have roving eyes for women while trying to keep up an image of happy family men. That research brought us to this fictional story...the story of a baby saved from possible harm by quietly sending her overseas, where—like her grandfather before her—she fought for women's rights, civil rights, and offered medical care for women and families in New York and Pennsylvania.

Fictional Bridie Mulholland brought the best of her genetic mix to a new land, smoothed and graded by her strong, faithful, and hardworking parents.

That made her a great character...and added a wonderful thread of history to a modern time when too many folks forget to appreciate the sacrifice and working hands that have toiled long and hard to shape our great nation.

SOMETHING DELICIOUS FROM A
Downhome Southern Kitchen

Tallie O'Meara isn't your everyday character. She's the salt-of-the-earth, hands-on woman who taught America's youth, directed a church choir, sewed costumes and choir robes, raised a family, and worked a job in a time when that was far from the norm.

Her faith and her family were her cornerstones, so it was a sad day when she was relieved of her choir duties...but our Tallie didn't pout! She stayed busy, changed churches, sang robustly, and made cookies—and her cookies were named the "Number One Very Best at the Northern Savannah Cookie Exchange," and that's something to be proud of. Unlike so many recipe hoarders, Tallie loves sharing her recipes and actually did a recipe file for each of her six granddaughters, based on her belief that a recipe is like a blessing...it needs to be shared to be appreciated. This is her double-batch recipe because doing a single batch would be just plain silly and shortsighted.

TALLIE'S FAMOUS SUGAR COOKIES & FROSTING!

Ingredients:

3 cups powdered sugar

2 cups butter, softened

2 eggs

1 teaspoon vanilla

1½ teaspoons almond extract

5 cups flour

2 teaspoons baking soda

Directions:

Cream together sugar, butter, eggs, and flavorings thoroughly until light and fluffy. Mix in flour and baking soda. While most recipes call for cream of tartar, Tallie is convinced that tartar should be left to teeth and nothing that should go into cookies, and she stood by that reasoning for a long, long time. Also, Tallie likes to use bread flour, but all-purpose flour works fine too. You just might want to add a little more of it, say a couple of tablespoons full.

Split dough into three equal-ish pieces. Wrap in plastic wrap, chill for an hour, and then roll out to cut out cookies one package at a time. Roll out to about 3/8" thick. (Too thin, and cookies get crispy. Part of the delight in Tallie's cookies is that they are crisp on the outside and chewy on the inside.) Cut out cookies and bake at 375 degrees for about 7 minutes...just until edges start to turn golden.

Cool.

Then frost with:

Tallie's Homemade Cookie Frosting

Ingredients:

1 cup butter, softened

6 cups powdered sugar

2 teaspoons almond extract

1 teaspoon vanilla extract

Splash of milk, just enough
to make spreadable.

Directions:

Mix all ingredients on low speed. When mixed, turn speed to high for about 3 minutes to fluff frosting.

Frost cookies. Decorate with sprinkles or sugars.

Enjoy!

*Read on for a sneak peek of another exciting book
in the Savannah Secrets series!*

Buried Secrets

BY GABRIELLE MEYER

Georgia Gazette
*Savannah, Georgia
January 7, 1785*

*It has come to the attention of your humble editor that
Rosewood Green, the estate abandoned by English loyalists in
the recent American War for Independence, has a new inhabi-
tant. His name will be familiar to one and all in Savannah for his
heroic efforts during the aforementioned war. But perhaps it will
also be familiar to several of Savannah's belles for reasons that
have nothing to do with military prowess.*

*Major General Absalom Tennent, formerly of New York,
has made his permanent home in our fair city after receiving
Rosewood Green as a gift from the Georgia State Assembly
for his gallant efforts in preserving the South during the war.
Along with his acquisition of Rosewood Green, Major General*

Tennent was awarded large tracts of land in North and South Carolina, but it is this editor's understanding that these gifts were sold to pay off debts the major general incurred during his time in the army.

For those who might be new to Savannah, I will take the liberty of sharing some of the more notorious exploits of our newest citizen. It will be up to you whether or not you think his gift was justified by our prestigious Assembly, although I think you will discover why I was against it from the start.

To begin our visit into the past, I think it is fair to say that the major general was not only successful in pushing General Cornwallis north into Virginia and overtaking the interior of South Carolina, thereby forcing the British to remain in Charleston for the duration of the war, but in claiming the hearts of countless young women wherever he marched. One might think this assessment unfair, given his illustrious heroism during the war and his close relationship with General George Washington, unless one's own daughter was a casualty of the major general's charms and misplaced affection, as was mine.

Upon Cornwallis's surrender, I was pleased to hear that Major General Tennent returned to his home state of New York. But, it's fair to say, based on several reputable news articles that have come across the Georgia Gazette's *desk, that the war did not diminish Major General Tennent's hunger for scandal. If one is to believe reports from New York, a rather intriguing affair unfolded just this past summer regarding our notorious hero. It seems that a young woman, of fair age and gracious upbringing, was embroiled in a scandalous liaison with the major general, one for which her father most heartily disapproved. When word reached her father that she had eloped with the aforementioned major general, her father tracked them down and forced an annulment, since his daughter was underage. The young woman was taken home and placed under constant supervision, to ensure she did not make the same mistake twice. But one wonders, was the damage already done? And does the young lady's father think she is safe? It is your humble editor's experience that she is not. Though the major general seems to have a penchant for willfully banishing these broken hearts from his short memory, the young ladies in question cannot so easily forget.*

Now that the major general has retired to his Savannah abode, is he ready to turn his sights on the unsuspecting fair maidens of this city?

Only time will tell the tale, but take heed and consider this fair warning: none of our wives, daughters, or sisters are immune to his charm or devastation.

It was one of those rare January days in Savannah when the temperature had risen above seventy degrees, and Meredith Bellefontaine wasn't about to waste it by staying indoors. With the new year almost a week old, she had decided to leave the Magnolia Investigations offices and walk across the street into Forsyth Park to do a little self-examination with the diary her daughter-in-law had given her for Christmas.

Though she had opened the diary and placed it on her lap with good intentions, she couldn't focus on the blank pages staring back at her. Instead, her gaze traveled around the park as she enjoyed the sights and sounds of people and animals taking advantage of the nice weather.

From her vantage point on a bench near the large Forsyth Fountain, she had a great view. Ancient oaks, laden with Spanish moss, arched over the large walkway leading up to the fountain. A couple of mothers, deep in conversation, pushed strollers while a jogger ran around them and an elderly couple, side by side on a neighboring bench, held hands in quiet companionship.

Meredith smiled, thinking about each of their stories, wondering what filled their days and hours. The older couple especially caught her attention. She had always thought that she and her late husband, Ron, would grow old together. Maybe pass their time in this way, side by side in a beautiful park. How could it be that he'd already been gone for two and a half years?

Shaking her head, Meredith sighed and looked back at her diary, slipping her curly blond hair behind one ear. Her daughter-in-law, Sherri Lynn, had asked her to start writing in the book, hoping

Meredith would record her life story for her grandchildren, Kaden and Kinsley. But where did she start? At the beginning?

She had her pen poised above the blank page when a new sight caught her attention. A funeral procession drove past on Whitaker Street, no doubt on their way to Laurel Grove North Cemetery. Dozens of cars followed a black hearse, their lights turned on in solidarity.

Meredith closed her eyes to say a prayer for the deceased's loved ones, remembering all too well the day they had buried Ron. She'd never known such grief. There were several people, including her son Carter, who had tried to convince her that enough time had passed since Ron's death for her to move on and find someone new—but she wasn't so sure. Could enough time ever pass?

"Meredith?" Arthur "Quin" Crowley's voice broke through Meredith's thoughts and prayers.

She opened her eyes, surprised to see him standing there. "Quin! What are you doing here?"

He smiled, his unique eyes—one blue and one brown—shining along with his smile. "I stopped by your office to talk to you, but Carmen said you were working in the park. She suggested I look for you here."

Carmen Lopez, Meredith's assistant, knew the pulse of the office better than anyone. She was a constant source of energy and creativity for Meredith and her business partner, Julia Foley. There were days that Meredith was convinced they couldn't run Magnolia Investigations without her.

Closing her diary, Meredith set it aside and patted the bench next to her. "Won't you join me?"

"Are you sure? I don't want to intrude on your quiet time. It looks like you were deep in thought."

Quin was a handsome man in his early sixties. His hair had turned silver, but his coloring suggested that it had been red at one time. He was trim and athletic and was usually dressed in business casual attire. His work as a lawyer kept him busy, though he was self-employed and set his own hours, leaving some free time to golf and volunteer. His thoughtfulness for others was one of his strongest traits.

"I was praying," she said to him as she looked at the tail end of the funeral procession. "For the family about to bury their loved one."

Quin glanced in the direction she had indicated, his gaze filling with understanding. His wife, Andrea, had died almost seven years ago.

"If you don't mind." He pointed to the bench. "I've actually come on business matters."

"Of course I don't mind." She moved over a little more to give him plenty of space.

He took a seat beside her, and she could smell the subtle cologne he wore. Their relationship had been a little uncertain over the past year and a half, though she suspected that if she gave him the green light, he'd be ready to move forward. But a nagging doubt often entered her heart whenever she thought about taking their relationship any further. They enjoyed each other's companionship and had many things in common, but was that enough? He'd been a gentleman and hadn't pressured her for more, for which she was grateful. Even if she wasn't ready to pursue a full-time relationship, she didn't want to say goodbye to him forever.

"What kind of business brings you to Magnolia Investigations?" she asked, putting aside her thoughts about their relationship for now.

Quin sighed, and his smiled disappeared. "Something has come up at the cemetery, and I was hoping you could help."

He had just taken over the presidency of the Colonial Park Cemetery board in January. The graveyard, which had been called Christ Church Cemetery during the colonial era, was the oldest in Savannah and one of the most visited by tourists. It was an honor to be voted president, and Meredith couldn't think of anyone more deserving of the position.

"What happened?" She sat up straighter and turned to face Quin on the bench, offering him her full attention.

"Someone broke into two of the old family vaults overnight, causing thousands of dollars' worth of damage. I had the police stop by this morning, when the vandalism was discovered, and they're on the case. They think it was a teenage prank or some kind of sorority initiation, but I have a feeling there's something else going on. I was wondering if I could hire Magnolia Investigations to do a little research to see if these vaults are connected in any way."

"Why would you think they were connected?"

"They're both about the same age, as far as I can tell—similar in style and construction. And they're both in the area with the earlier plots but not right next to each other. If it had been a teenage prank, don't you think the kids would have vandalized two vaults in close proximity? These aren't even in view of each other."

"Really?" Meredith's mind was already turning with questions. She was familiar with the cemetery, from a tour guide's perspective, but didn't know much about the actual people buried there. "Can Julia and I stop by and take a look?"

"That's what I was hoping." Quin smiled. "I've also called my sister-in-law, Rosalyn, to head up here. She's a forensic anthropologist from the University of Florida. She can't get here until Monday with her team of graduate students, so we're going to keep the vaults open over the weekend. The police put up tape and cordoned off the area, and the cemetery caretaker is putting a guard on duty to make sure no one else tampers with the vaults."

Meredith was intrigued. "What do you think happened? If it wasn't a teenage prank, why do you think someone broke into the vaults?"

Quin shook his head. "I really don't have any idea. Some of the vaults have been empty since the Civil War when Union soldiers opened them and stole anything of value. Others are inhabited, but their occupants' names and information are forever lost to history. Still others that are believed to be the final resting place of war heroes, famous Georgians, and prominent Savannah citizens have been opened over the years, only to discover that the people they thought were inside were not. The cemetery is full of unanswered mysteries. Why would someone open up two different vaults without a purpose?"

A gentle warm breeze brushed against Meredith's cheeks as she thought about Quin's words. He was right. The cemetery had a long and complicated history, but there had been little research done on it over the years. There were more questions than answers and little funding to look for them.

"I can't speak for Julia, but I would love to do what I can." Meredith smiled at Quin, hoping she could be helpful to him and the cemetery board. "But I'll ask her, and I have a feeling she'll be just as curious as I am."

"Thank you. I've been the board president for less than a week. I'd hate to disappoint anyone who voted for me." He reached out and put his hand on hers. It was large and firm but gentle. "It means a lot to me, Meredith."

She looked down at their hands, loving the way it felt to have someone show her warm affection. She waited for that catch in her conscience, the one that usually pricked her whenever she felt any sort of attraction to another man since Ron's death, but she didn't feel it this time. Yet—she wasn't quite ready to return the affection, so she pulled her hand back and picked up her diary and pen and then rose to her feet.

Quin also stood.

"I don't have anything pressing on my calendar this afternoon," she said to him. "I'll walk back to the office and see if Julia is available to head over to the cemetery now."

"Mind if I walk with you?"

She shook her head. "Of course not."

As they walked back to the agency, Meredith's mind was awhirl with thoughts of Colonial Cemetery—and Quin Crowley.

A Note from the Editors

WE HOPE YOU ENJOY THE Savannah Secrets series, created by the Books and Inspirational Media Division of Guideposts, a nonprofit organization that touches millions of lives every day through products and services that inspire, encourage, help you grow in your faith, and celebrate God's love in every aspect of your daily life.

Thank you for making a difference with your purchase of this book, which helps fund our many outreach programs to military personnel, prisons, hospitals, nursing homes, and educational institutions. To learn more, visit GuidepostsFoundation.org.

We also maintain many useful and uplifting online resources. Visit Guideposts.org to read true stories of hope and inspiration, access OurPrayer network, sign up for free newsletters, download free e-books, join our Facebook community, and follow our stimulating blogs.

To learn about other Guideposts publications, including the bestselling devotional *Daily Guideposts*, go to ShopGuideposts.org, call (800) 932-2145, or write to Guideposts, PO Box 5815, Harlan, Iowa 51593.

Sign up for the
Guideposts Fiction Newsletter
and stay up-to-date on the books you love!

You'll get sneak peeks of new releases, recommendations from other Guideposts readers, and special offers just for you . . .
and it's FREE!

Just go to Guideposts.org/Newsletters
today to sign up.

Guideposts®

**Visit Guideposts.org/Shop
or call (800) 932-2145**

Find more inspiring stories in these best-loved Guideposts fiction series!

Mysteries of Lancaster County

Follow the Classen sisters as they unravel clues and uncover hidden secrets in Mysteries of Lancaster County. As you get to know these women and their friends, you'll see how God brings each of them together for a fresh start in life.

Secrets of Wayfarers Inn

Retired schoolteachers find themselves owners of an old warehouse-turned-inn that is filled with hidden passages, buried secrets, and stunning surprises that will set them on a course to puzzling mysteries from the Underground Railroad.

Tearoom Mysteries Series

Mix one stately Victorian home, a charming lakeside town in Maine, and two adventurous cousins with a passion for tea and hospitality. Add a large scoop of intriguing mystery, and sprinkle generously with faith, family, and friends, and you have the recipe for *Tearoom Mysteries*.

Ordinary Women of the Bible

Richly imagined stories—based on facts from the Bible—have all the plot twists and suspense of a great mystery, while bringing you fascinating insights on what it was like to be a woman living in the ancient world.

To learn more about these books, visit Guideposts.org/Shop